Valley

of

Hemlock

EDEN REED

A New Leaf Book
Published by WigWam Publishing Co.
P.O. Box 6992
Villa Park, IL 60181
http://www.newleafbooks.net

Copyright © 1999, 2016 by Teresa A. Basile
Library of Congress Catalogue Card Number: 99-67671
ISBN 10: 1-930076-25-8
ISBN 13: 978-1-930076-25-9

Printed in the U.S.A.

I do not often speak ill of the dead. Life is a fragile, sacred trust and should be honored as such regardless of how the life was led. But when evil overpowers the will of good, a wickedness so strong that the spirit endures long after the flesh, I can only believe that this life was truly evil. The evil of which I speak resided in Boothe House.

In the months that passed I often wondered if I were destined to become part of its legacy or if it were some trick of fate that cast me upon its doorstep. What transpired there whether it was real or imagined would always be a part of my existence and taint my reverence in faith. If only I knew then....

❧ ONE ❧

I was nineteen when I committed my first murder. Having never harmed another person before, the prospect terrified me. For days my conscience agonized over the possible consequences. But what else could I do? Harold had to die, and only I could do it.

After gearing up my courage I finished the deed. A smile of satisfaction followed. I was aghast at what I had done and yet … pleased. According to the numerous letters I received, so were my readers.

With the stroke of a pen, I created adventure, intrigue and romantic love—things I loved most to dream about. With a gift of imagination I became the beautiful heroine whose poise and grace captured the heart of the dashing hero in chapter two. By chapter twelve, I foiled the villain with my cunning wit and razor perception.

The power became intoxicating.

Many books followed. My novels became a treasured commodity in the world of the gentle set. Success was mine to savor, but the taste was bittersweet; there was no one to share it.

Someone accused me once of becoming too dependent on my fictional world. There are different views of reality, I explained. You can accept what is presented as is, or you can search for a more favorable angle. I chose to search. My father called this "assertive intelligence." Of course, when I refused to accept his angle he called me just plain "stubborn." Like father like daughter I would say.

As a stalwart military man, tall of frame and solid in stature, my father was an imposing figure on and off the field. A commander of the first order, a brilliant strategist, the Colonel had the ability to reduce an opponent to a bumbling mass of quaking nerves with a mere cast of his hardened eye.

To an awkward girl of fifteen, however, who sat alone and overlooked at the dance, this gruff soldier with the dark silver whiskers was an endearing knight, an amusing ally, a champion. With a gentle nudge and whispers of encouragement, he brightened my spirits and coaxed out a smile.

I never outgrew those awkward years, nor, thankfully, did I outgrow the strength of his wisdom and sometimes-opinionated advice. Oh, he could still raise the gooseflesh on my arms when I invoked his displeasure, but I never felt more needed or loved those years after my mother died.

The Colonel was proud of my work though he didn't view my writing as serious journalism. He often pined for grandchildren and suggested I lay down my pen and marry the butcher. Although the amiable little man was probably my best prospect for a wedded future, his pug like attributes and heavy garlic cologne did not fit the mold of dashing hero.

Again, I was stubborn.

My work continued to be well received, but I disparaged over mediocrity. The walks through Hyde Park no longer held the inspiration I sought, nor did the soft hum of Lucille's motor as I drove around the channels of Oxfordshire. There was little left in my familiar world to stimulate the fresh approach for which I yearned. Frustrated and unable to record a single decent thought, marriage to the butcher didn't seem so bad.

Drastic measures were in order.

Though I had never been to Hemlock the name itself aroused my curiosity. The small advertisement for Boothe House proclaimed to be the perfect solution. The sprawling estate with bountiful gardens and tranquil accommodations sounded like the ideal haven for someone in need—someone like me.

As with all of my stories, I started with a question. As I stowed my suitcases in Lucille's rear compartment, a question finally came to mind uniquely suited to my coming situation: When a woman is alone among strangers, whom does she trust? So remarkable in simplicity, yet rich with possibilities. I set off on my journey assured in the knowledge that my slump was at an end.

My instincts never steered me wrong.

The valley welcomed my arrival with sweeping arms of grey mist and roads that led nowhere. When the same pub fell under the glow of Lucille's headlights for a third time, I tossed my ill-printed map to the back and pulled to a stop. A cold rush of air seeped through my thin silk blouse and knee-length skirt. Pulling on my overcoat, I shivered, then chided myself for not dressing appropriately for the unpredictable northern clime. Fog, thick and damp, swirled against my feet as I hurried to the entrance. The weather beaten sign over the door swung on rusty chains. Croakers was its name, an establishment full of good cheer and good ale, if the ribald sounds of merriment were any indication.

The air inside, laden with tobacco fumes and liquor, hung as heavy as the fog outside. Heat from the great stone fireplace washed my face in welcome. The reception I received, however, was less than cordial.

Before the door had even closed behind me, the camaraderie of the patrons broke off to a hushed whisper. Each man in turn set his lips to a grim line and eyed the stranger who came in from the cold.

I cleared my throat and nodded. "Hello."

Their silence unnerved me. I was discouraged but not surprised. My research of Hemlock had indicated how, as a small farming village, the residents were private people who thrived on custom and avoided change. And unfamiliar women, I noted.

"Pay them no mind," said a sturdy middle-aged woman from behind the bar. Streaks of grey peaked out from under the handkerchief on her head and her girth was as ample as her smile. She wiped the thick cherry wood counter with one hand and pointed a thumb toward the men with the other. "They don't mean any harm. They just tend to get overprotective about their meetings. Huh, you'd think it were a matter of national security," she scoffed with a roll of her eyes.

"Well, go on with ya," she shouted toward the men who still stared at me as if I were contagion. "She's not here to spy on yer secret manure recipe, Seamus." With a quick turn of her head she asked, "Are you?"

"No," I promptly replied. As intriguing as manure harvesting sounded, the idea was the farthest thing from my mind. Their secret, I assured them, was safe with me.

As the men grudgingly returned to their communal, the woman straightened her apron and leaned her elbows on the bar. "So what can I get you?" she asked. Her dark hazel eyes scrutinized my rumpled overcoat and disheveled hair. "You look like you could stand a pot of tea."

Directions to Boothe House were what I really needed, but tea sounded heavenly. And a few stolen moments to examine the backbone of Hemlock would serve me well. "Tea would be lovely," I replied. I shrugged out of my coat, took a seat on a stool and absorbed the rustic charm surrounding me.

The pub was constructed with cherry paneled walls and rough-hewn ceiling beams darkened with age but with a luster of strength and stability. A coat of arms hung over the mantel festooned with a lion and a lamb; a collection of sculptured whalebone steins, antique lures and decoys decorated one wall, a Scott's pipes and a knight's sword and hauberk another—all treasures of lives that once had been. It wasn't hard to envision generations of townsfolk gathering here to swap their joys and sorrows.

The woman returned with a pot and two cups. After pouring

a cup for me she poured one for herself and doused it with a liberal amount of brandy. She lifted the bottle in offering, but I declined. On an empty stomach, brandy would likely go right to my head. "Finding the road in this fog is difficult enough," I replied. "I've been driving in circles for the past hour already."

"You must be from the city," she said.

I nodded. "Am I that obvious?"

She gave a conspiratorial wink. "That contraption you arrived in is a dead give-away. We don't have any machines like that around here." She motioned to where my pale yellow roadster rested just beyond the window. "Is it safe?"

"Oh, Lucille? She's perfectly safe."

"Lucille is it? It even has a name?"

"I consider her to be more of a companion than a mode of transportation," I explained.

"A young woman, far from home, traveling alone should have more than a machine for a companion," she said with a cluck of her tongue.

"That's what my father said," I replied, still hearing the deep pitch of authority in the Colonel's voice as he tried to dissuade me. "But I appealed to his sense of adventure."

"Adventure," she scoffed. "I've lived here all of my life and never regretted a minute of it."

"Not ever?"

"Well …" She gave a wink. "Almost never. I look at the same old faces every day and hear the same old stories. And sometimes …" She turned a rosy smile to me. "… a pretty new face stops in from time to time and it's a welcomed change. Strangers are sparse this time of year."

"So I gathered," I said, still aware of the occasional glare from the members of the taproom.

She gave a little snort in the direction of the men. "They'll be getting to their voting soon and then they'll go on home."

True to her word, a gavel struck the mantel calling for silence in the room. All eyes centered on the burly man with a sandy beard and moustache standing erect by the hearth.

"Let's get to the business at hand," he began. "You all know that the Widow Bradley's barn is in need of repair. Winter's coming and she'll need a sturdy shelter for her ewes. It will take but a day for us to repair. I'll hear the yea votes now."

A chorus of "yea" answered him.

"Nays?" None came. "Done." The gavel struck again. "Tomorrow is the fifteenth of October." He hesitated a moment, his eyes creasing with sadness. "We all remember sweet Alicia Mae. We pray for her soul and denounce the evil that led her to take her own life."

A man in the back began to rise, his voice slurred and strained with emotion. "The devil took my little girl! I'll make him pay. I swear I will." As two men settled him gently back in his chair, tears ran down his face. "Make him pay, I will," he mumbled, somehow knowing his quest was a useless cause. I questioned the woman with a raise of one eyebrow. She mouthed, "That's her father."

That answered my first question, but curiosity was getting the better of me. Who was Alicia Mae and why did she choose to end her life? Was it for love? Or desperation?

"For flowers to be placed on her grave, I'll hear the yeas now." Yeas answered morosely and just as before the nays were silent. "Done." The gavel struck again. The men finished their ale in gulped unison and bade their farewells.

I waited until the majority had left before I began my interrogation. "Did Alicia Mae live here in the village?" I asked quietly.

The woman nodded the corners of her mouth downcast. "She grew up here. It was a tragedy, it was."

"What happened to her?"

The woman raised her head in fond reflection. "Alicia Mae was a pretty little thing, always liked to be in the center of things, always looking to better herself. She was a bit spirited, if you know what I mean." The woman leaned over the counter to whisper. "She had a roving eye. There was a bit of a falling out with her intended over that. Then three weeks before the wedding they found her floating in the lake. A suicide, they said. There are those who say otherwise."

"You mean she was murdered?"

She straightened and shrugged her shoulders. "The truth may never be known. Charlie, her father, the dear man, swears that Alicia would never take her own life. Maybe the falling out was a bit more serious than supposed."

"So you think her fiancé did it?"

"I don't think much on it anymore. Charlie does, though. Of course, who could blame him, her being found on his property and all?"

"Was there any evidence …?"

She shook her head. "No, none could be found. That's the grief of it. I guess it's hard for a father to accept the fact that his only child would take her own life. Poor Charlie. It's been three years now. I don't think he'll ever accept it."

"How sad," I reflected aloud.

The woman nodded in agreement. "That it is. But enough about lover's quarrels and people dying. I don't want you to leave here thinking Hemlock such a sorry place."

"Oh, I don't," I assured her. "I wouldn't be staying here if I did."

"You're staying here? In Hemlock?" Her cheeks dimpled with a smile.

"Yes, I've rented a room at Boothe House. Do you know where I can find it?"

The color suddenly drained from her face. Her husband approached with a tray of soiled glasses he gathered from the now empty tables. They exchanged worried glances.

Had I said something wrong?

"But that's—" she began. Her husband shot her a look; a look one might mistake for a warning.

"Is there something wrong?" I prodded.

"Well, no," she said hesitantly, "we just didn't realize his lordship was taking in boarders is all."

"Most manor houses do these days. To help pay for the upkeep."

"Will you be staying long?" Her eyes strayed back to her husband to see if he was still about. Noting he was still within earshot, she pursed her lips in vexation.

"Only a few months," I answered. "Just long enough to finish my book."

"So you're a writer then?"

I nodded. "Trying to be anyway. I'm hoping some peace and quiet will inspire me."

"Well, you'll find a good deal to write about up there—"

"Aggie!" her husband interrupted. "It's time to close up."

I took my cue and gathered my purse. I wanted to be on my way anyway, anxious for a long hot soak and a bite of something delicious from the master kitchen at Boothe House. "How much do I owe you for the tea?"

"Nothing, Miss. Consider it a welcome gift."

"Thank you. That's very kind. And please call me Meredith, Meredith Barlow."

"I'm Aggie Towns," she offered. "And this is Duff."

Her husband paused in his washing of glasses to nod but declined to share even a hint of approval.

"I guess I should be going. It doesn't look like the fog will lift anytime soon. Is it this way?" I pointed to the road leading north.

She nodded. "Take the road about a quarter mile. When you see the signpost pointing left, turn right. The entrance is just off the road. You can't miss it."

But I almost did. Lucille's headlights, more of a hindrance than help, reflected against the thick fog casting odd caricatures of human shapes before me. For a split second I thought I had seen a hunchbacked man stumble before me. I swerved to miss him, throwing mud and gravel in my haste to stop. I immediately got out of the car to see if I had hit him. There was nothing there. No body. No sign of tragedy. No pleas for help.

Strange. Nothing moved. Nothing made a sound.

I felt very silly for having imagined the whole thing; yet, a disquieting sense of alarm told me it wasn't just a figment of my imagination.

Stilling my racing heart, I walked back to Lucille. The crunch of stones beneath each step sounded eerily out of place. Too quiet. The growing suspicion that there was something else Aggie wanted to tell me plagued my mind. Her husband, it seemed, as with the rest of the men, didn't take kindly to strangers. But I had made one friend in Aggie, and that was the first step. I made a mental note to return to the pub soon to find out what Aggie was hiding.

I noticed it then, the tall wrought iron arch with the name Boothe House cast above. The gates hung wide open, rusted in place. As I turned onto the drive, fog thinned and the mist advanced to a steady rhythmic rain. The road felt rough and sluggish as Lucille crept up the steep uneven path. I rounded a bend where the landscape encroached upon the road. Unattended trees and bramble snatched out at Lucille's doors and rooftop. There was no evidence of the well-manicured lawns I envisioned. It was quite the contrary; the unkempt grounds had grown wild with neglect. What other surprises lay in store for me, I wondered.

The next bend was more treacherous. Lucille slid past the parameters of the road and became stuck. Her back wheels spun aimlessly. With every attempt I made to loosen her, she sank deeper into the mud. "Blast it all!" I cursed aloud. Not that anyone could hear me. I sat on a desolate road on a stormy night. No one would be able to hear me curse the devil himself let alone call for help. But I didn't want to dwell on that thought.

I had two choices: I could stay in the cold confines of Lucille and hope that someone would come looking for me or I could complete my trip on foot. Rumblings from my stomach and shivers along my skin decided for me. I loved Lucille dearly, but she was a poor replacement for a soft, dry bed and warm food.

Climbing out, I went quickly to the rear compartment to retrieve my things. Cold, wet mud oozed over the sides of my new brown pumps. I gritted my teeth and stifled the urge to cry. "Buck up!" I said to myself. "You've been in worse spots." Of course, I couldn't think of any at the moment.

As I stood there fumbling with my umbrella I heard a distinct snapping of twigs. Thank heavens, I thought. I've been saved.

"Hello? Is anyone there? I seem to be stuck."

No one answered. Rain patted my eyelashes and dripped down my cheeks. "Hello?" I called again, only now my voice sounded strained and wary.

Silence. The same disquieting silence that had greeted me at the gates.

"Your imagination is working overtime," I mumbled to myself, dismissing the idea that the sounds I heard were anything but my imagination. "Just keep moving. The sooner you get to the house, the sooner you can dry off and hopefully wash these expensive shoes you insisted on buying."

As I pulled the smaller of my two suitcases from the compartment I paused, just realizing I had spoken my thoughts out loud. "And now you're talking to yourself." I was hungry. I always babbled when I got hungry.

It came again: the sound of footsteps breaking through the tangled brush as if someone or something were tracking me. And for me to hear it over the pelting rain, it would have to be quite near.

I slammed down the compartment door. The rest of my things would have to wait. With a suitcase in one hand and an umbrella in the other, I took to the road and listened to see if I was being followed. The sounds of movement came first from the left then the right. Or was it the right then the left? The rain and darkness confused me. A forest of trees banked each side of the road that seemed to have no end. My arm began to ache from the weight of my suitcase.

My stomach gurgled again. How much farther could it be?

A branch snapped behind me. I whirled around to confront my tracker, umbrella poised for attack. "Who are y—?"

The accusation died on my lips. It wasn't what I saw, but what I heard that made my lungs fill with a gasp. The voice was hushed, almost to a whisper, but the meaning was perfectly distinct.

"*You don't belong here.*"

Breath—or was it just the wind?—brushed across my neck. Spinning in circles, I tried to lock sight on the phantom. Had someone followed me from Croakers? Rain dribbled down my forehead blurring my vision. I wiped my eyes across my sleeve. "If this is a joke, I fail to see the humor." The void of darkness encircled me. "If you're trying to frighten me, I can assure you it's a useless cause. I don't scare easily." That was a complete and utter lie. Bluff when you can, my father taught me and never let them sense your fear.

But I was afraid. Afraid of what lurked out there plotting my demise. The wind picked up. Branches overhead began to groan and creek. The sound was a laugh, a jeer, a sigh. Could that have been what I heard? The sob of the trees in the wind?

A giggle bubbled up from somewhere deep in my sense of the ridiculous. Not just a mild titter, but a full-blown laugh of relief. I had been so eager to devise the perfect plot for my next book that I had transformed my surroundings into a sinister villain. Neither a maniacal lunatic nor hungry nocturnal animals were chasing me; I was composing an element of fear that would do any mystery novel proud. Yes, that was it. The stimulus of a good rainstorm at night always evoked an aura of suspense. I would have to remember every detail right down to the chill still coursing down my spine.

My feet moved on of their own accord, a little faster perhaps than before, but sure and steady. The stalking sounds disappeared and were replaced by echoes of rain tapping against the top of the umbrella.

The trees parted into a clearing. "Finally," I breathed. A hot bath, clean crisp sheets and a toasty warm fire awaited me. All that worrying for naught.

After I convinced myself I had nothing else to fear, I took my first glimpse of Boothe House ... and nearly screamed.

❧ TWO ❧

Lightening spread its tentacles across the sky illuminating the house and all its ghastly shadows.

It was a massive brick and stone Tudor-style structure with spires piercing the ominous clouds. It must have been grand in its day, but evidence of decay was clearly visible. As I approached the entrance, I wondered if I had taken a wrong turn. I didn't have the strength to walk any farther. The wide front steps were broken and uneven. Pieces of the intricate cornice lay in a bed of twisted vines. The head of a griffin, fallen from the encasement around the door, lay in pieces at my feet.

Doubts grew rapidly in my mind. In big, bold letters the name Boothe was carved in the granite over the entrance. So this was going to be my home for the next two months. I didn't know if I should be relieved or mortified. Where was the grand manor I had read about?

The iron knocker was cold and stiff. When my efforts received no response I tried the latch. The door swung open with a barely audible creak.

"Hello?"

The doubts that had begun to fester were now serious deliberations as I stepped into the entrance at Boothe House. Every house has a feel to it. It's transformed by the people who live there. It makes you feel warm and welcome or uncomfortable and unwanted.

I wanted to run.

That strange eerie silence again, as if all sound was forbidden to be heard. The house sensed my presence and objected to it. It was a ridiculous notion; surely I was just letting my experience on the road cloud my judgement for no house could actually form an opinion—only people do—or so I thought.

Clock chimes punctured my trance. Nine o'clock. It had been a very long and exhausting day. Hell house or no, I was going to get out of my sopping wet clothes and into a nice warm bed. I set down my suitcase, closed the door behind me, folded my umbrella and slipped out of my sodden, now ruined shoes.

"Hello?" Where was everybody?

Oil lamps pasted a yellow glow along the walls. A pair of double doors stood closed off to the left. Down that same hall several more rooms appeared closed and abandoned. In the middle, a large staircase ascended to a second floor swathed in darkness. To the right a faint light from under one door drew my attention. Someone was still awake.

I knocked softly before trying the latch. The well-oiled hinges barely made a sound when I entered.

A smile of praise was hard to resist. Here was a comfortable room; one that looked to be used and appreciated, a library or music room perhaps for there was a grand piano covered with a dust sheet near the window. A dying fire crackled in the hearth dispersing the chill in the air and atmosphere. Standing before it, I raised my hands to its heat and sighed with pleasure as the warmth penetrated my skin.

The room was quite large and smelled of leather and ink. Shadows danced upon the many rows of books lining the walls. And so many books there were. Home at last.

My eyes scanned the perimeter of the room. Though I appeared to be alone, I sensed I wasn't. I was being watched, my every move scrutinized.

The voice was unfamiliar but the words I remembered all too well.

"You don't belong here."

be, well, owned by an old man. "Then if you would be so kind as to refund the money I forwarded."

"I'll have a draft drawn up tomorrow."

There was no discussion of the matter, no barter for better terms. Now I was in a quandary with no other place to go. Like all good soldiers under my father's tutelage I advanced my troops. "Since a room is still paid for until my refund is received, I'm sure you won't mind if I avail myself to one of your rooms for tonight. You may deduct it from what is due me. As you can see it is raining quite heavily; the roads are washed out and Lucille is stuck in the mud."

"There's someone with you?"

The look of horror on his face was almost comical. If I hadn't been in such a dire predicament I would have indulged in the humor of it; but like Lucille, I was losing ground and quickly. "No. Lucille is my motorcar."

He wasn't amused. His dark brow creased to a straight, unbroken line. Perhaps spending the night with Lucille wasn't such a bad idea after all. I turned to leave.

"Where do you think you're going?" he said, just as I reached the front door.

"Outside where there's more hospitable conditions." I spat over my shoulder. Dead leaves whipped into a frenzy across my stocking feet as I opened the door. No shoes. *Blast it all!* An expensive pair of ruined shoes thwarted what promised to be a grand departure.

Rain splattered the threshold. A hand reached over my shoulder and closed the door. He sighed, whether resignation or disgust I couldn't be sure. "You'll go nowhere tonight," he said in a low voice very near my ear, melting a pinch of my hostility. "I suppose it's the least I can do for having 'acquainted' myself with you in the library."

He mocked me. Was my inexperience so transparent? I may not have resembled a woman born to sophisticated pleasures but I was educated and well read in the ways of the world. "You're too kind," I retorted, barely concealing the rancor I felt.

A crook of a smile lifted his lips. His shoulder brushed mine as he bent to retrieve my suitcase. He stood uncomfortably close to me again, only now I found the proximity quite loathsome. "You may take whatever room you like though you probably won't find any suitable. They haven't been used in years."

"Thank you," I replied, grabbing my suitcase from his outstretched hand. "I'm sure one will be adequate."

Taking his nod as a sign of dismissal, I headed for the staircase. His voice halted me on the third step. "Tomorrow when the roads are clear you will have to find other accommodations."

"I shall count the hours," I mumbled as I mounted the stairs. I thought myself unheard until I caught the hint of a grin in his "good night."

After my first encounter with Lord Boothe, I didn't expect him to do the gentlemanly thing and show me upstairs. And he didn't. I found the wing of guestrooms on my own. When I opened each door, I found that the irritating man was right. Cobwebs blanketed the first bedroom; holes littered the draperies and quilts where moths had eaten away the fine threads. The stuffiness made my nose twitch.

The next bedroom was in much the same condition. I was about to resign myself to the lesser of the two evils when I found myself being propelled down to the end of the corridor. Another room sat apart from the main hallway, its door hidden from view. A light blazed through the open portal. I descended the two steps cautiously for fear of intruding on someone's privacy. The room was empty.

A few cold ashes lay undisturbed in the hearth. A small lamp burned brightly on a table near the bedside. It was a large but cozy room and quite feminine. The draperies and matching comforter were a lovely shade of lavender with a print of forest green vines entwining themselves along the lace border. And not one moth-eaten hole. The wallpaper, though yellowed with aged, displayed the same vines giving me the feeling of standing in the midst of an enchanted garden.

There was a separate dressing room and private bath. Though there was no fire I felt warm and welcomed. The stir of creativity began to flow. Maybe I had judged this place too quickly. I was beginning to have misgivings, but as I looked at the large inviting four-poster, the lace pillows, and especially the Chippendale writing desk, I knew I was home. Even if only for one night.

Odd. The room appeared unoccupied. The armoire stood empty, and there was a thick layer of dust on the top of the writing table, yet I got the distinct impression that the room had been inhabited and quite recently.

The dressing room held a mirror stand and a dressing table. Small, round, crystal vials sat neatly in a row on top. The largest of the vials held a unique perfume: sweet ginger, the most pleasant fragrance I had ever experienced. I replaced the vial, careful not to disturb its outline in the dust.

As I passed the corner mirror I shrieked. My neatly coifed hair clung to my head with errant locks dripping down my neckline. Circles were beginning to form under my eyes making them look overly round and gaunt. I blanched, understanding Lord Boothe's aversion at finding such a ghastly looking creature in his arms.

One moment I was looking at my face and then at his. His sudden reflection in the mirror startled me. He stood behind me in the open doorway. I had forgotten to close the door.

"How did you get in here?"His ferocious look was most unnerving. He must practice in the mirror, I thought. He had the ultimate of intimidation down perfectly.

"The door was open and there didn't seem to be anyone occupying it …"

"This door has been locked for over twenty years!"

He insinuated things about my character again that I didn't take kindly to. "If it was locked as you say, then how did I get in? Having just arrived I wouldn't possibly know where the key is, would I? Or even have time to look for it. Now if you'll excuse me, I'm really very tired and would like to go to bed." I cast my attention to unpacking my suitcase. Stubbornness was sometimes a virtue.

"I'm sure you'll be more comfortable in another room."

"I've seen some of the other rooms and no, I will not. You did say I had my choice?" At his nod I felt a little sliver of triumph. "Then this is the room I choose. I promise not to disturb anything if that is your worry."

His expression softened somewhat, and I caught a glimpse of the charming rogue inside of that brusque exterior. I imagined many young women falling prey to this ruse.

"My only worry is for your welfare, Miss Barlow. This section of the house is unsafe."

"This room appears to be perfectly safe, and someone else must have thought so, too, or the door would not have been open." I paused then—a brief thought entered my mind, a very disturbing thought. "There *are* other residents in the house, aren't there?"

The one corner of his mouth lifted in a wry smile at my obvious concern for my virtue. The eyes that just moments ago were accusing me of treason were now laughing at the faint blush across my cheeks. "Yes, there are other 'residents'. There are two in the physical sense: a cook and a housekeeper. But I'm not sure how many actual 'residents' roam the halls."

"Are you trying to tell me that this house is haunted?" I was beginning to tire of people trying to scare me.

His features turned hard again without warning. "That is the rumor."

"If you're trying to frighten me, sir, you are wasting your time. I no more believe in ghosts than in flying pigs. So if you are finished, I'd like to retire. As you've been so gracious in allowing me to stay the night, I'd like to spend the rest of it sleeping."

"My intent is not to frighten you Miss Barlow only to

persuade you. I would still prefer that you move to a different room."

Why was this man objecting so to my staying in this room? Did he have some perverse desire to see me surrounded in cobwebs and moths? I knew he could sense my nervousness, was even feeding on it, but I was not going to give him the satisfaction of seeing me back down. "You said I could have any room I choose. I chose this one. Now, unless you are going back on your word, I will remain here." I knew that when it came to a question of honor most men did not like to be challenged. Lord Boothe was no exception. He left with the same frown with which he had come.

Victory. You would think after having bested such a difficult adversary, I would be filled with smug satisfaction. Then why were my hands shaking? Ghosts certainly didn't frighten me. Haunted indeed! I didn't believe it for a second. The man himself was more frightening than his tales. Frightening? Yes, I was frightened of him and the way he made me feel. I loathed him with an intensity that scared the wits out of me. It was just my weariness taking hold, I told myself. Things would look different after a good night's rest.

I closed the door, turned the lock and found the subject of our quarrel in the palm of my hand: the key. It had been there all the time on the inside of the door. Had Lord Boothe found it, I don't know how I would have explained my ignorance. Timing and luck, it seemed, had finally teamed to my side.

My appetite had completely vanished. So did my desire for a hot sudsy bath. All I really wanted was to climb into bed, close my eyes, and forget what a nightmare the day had become.

Wearing a fresh, dry nightgown and with my hair only mildly damp, I blew out the lamp, climbed into the big four-poster and under the quilted comforter. I lay there staring up at the ceiling listening intently for any unusual bumps in the night. When the possibility of a ghost is mentioned whether it is believed or not, one still wonders.

Off in the distance the mantel clock struck ten as my ensuing slumber took hold. A cool breeze brushed across my cheek. I instinctively pulled the comforter closer about my neck. Lingering there in a half-sleep, I wondered how a clock in a room supposedly locked for twenty years could still keep time. I never came up with an answer—the scent of sweet ginger claimed my attention as a beautiful woman entered my dreams.

❧ THREE ❦

She sat at the desk in my garden room. In her hand rested a letter that would never be delivered. The words of heartache she had written crumpled to a ball in the palm of her hand. Her shoulders slumped to the desk as she gave vent to her sorrow and wept. So sad, so desperately sad was she.

The realness of the vision alarmed me. She carried me through her torment of once experiencing true happiness and knowing it would never come again. There was more than a cloud of sadness lingering over her— there was also fear. A fear of losing something very dear to her heart.

The door opened. A small, dark-haired boy with an exquisite little upturned face entered the room, and immediately her mood lightened. With opened arms she gathered the child to her, reveling in the closeness they so seldom shared. They laughed and played, but all too soon it was time to say good-bye. She stood in the doorway; a parting smile upon her lips; waving at the motorcar that took away the child and her only reason for living.

I awoke the next morning feeling I had slept very little. The dream resembled more of a nightmare than the imaginative pondering a restive sleep can bring. Given the setting I was in, I was not surprised. Boothe House had a way of conjuring up many disturbing thoughts. But there was little time to dwell on it. As it was made abundantly clear to me the night before, I needed to find other accommodations.

Rain still trickled down the panes of glass that separated me from the oppressive sky. My wardrobe for the day was more practical; a pair of slacks and calf high boots were less in vogue than my silk suit but more appropriate for sloshing about in the mud and wet. If I had to walk all the way back to the village, I wanted to be prepared. Most villages had a room or two to rent to weary travelers, and I hoped Hemlock was one of them. I would try Croakers first, for I sensed I would need the help of my one and only ally, Aggie Towns.

My stomach twisted and churned, rumbling its protest for not having been fed. I left the sanctity of my garden room to venture down to the kitchen in hopes of stealing a morsel or two. Now I would have an opportunity to see what the house was truly like.

Boothe House was no less intimidating in the morning light, what little light there was, that is. The oil lamps were still turned down low, a conscious effort to control costs, I guessed. I squinted to make out the smaller details, but from what I could see time had not been an ally. The house had all the air and feel of a century gone by, and looked as if a century had come and gone; chunks of ceiling plaster had fallen; the wallpaper had become brittle and slivered pieces fell at the slightest touch. It was eighteenth century elaborate with a good deal of potential. It could be a fine showplace if it had a mind to. But did it have a mind to?

"You are late, Miss Barlow," I heard his voice call out as I passed the informal dining room.

I winced. What could I possibly be late for? My departure? "Pardon me?"

Lord Boothe stopped in his eating to give me his perusal. His eyes started with my face, then moved down my dark blue sweater to my grey wool trousers. A flush of heat rose to my cheeks. Never before had I felt so self-conscious about my appearance—or lack of one. I looked quite different, I supposed, from the previous night. Whether he approved of the transformation or not was unreadable. I didn't know why that should have mattered to me, but it did.

"You're late," he repeated. "Breakfast is served at eight o'clock. If you would please take your seat."

Breakfast? He nodded to the chair to his left. My stomach answered his invitation with a low rumbling growl. As I took the offered seat a thin austere looking woman entered. Her uniform matched her solid grey hair that was pulled into a tight bun. She was small in size, almost child-like but carried a heavy coffee urn in one hand with ease, never spilling a drop.

"Miss Barlow will be joining me after all, Linnea. Please see that she is served," Lord Boothe instructed.

"Yes, sir," the woman replied. She cast a wary eye in my direction before heading back to the kitchen. She returned moments later with poached eggs and thin slices of ham. Cold. I concluded by the smug little smile she wore that I got precisely what I deserved for my tardiness.

We talked briefly through breakfast in what would be considered polite conversation. My host conducted himself pleasantly, our encounter from the previous night having been forgotten for the most part. By him, anyway. I, on the other hand, could not keep my mind off of the kiss and how shamelessly I allowed it. I fidgeted with my napkin, as I often do when feeling at a disadvantage. No matter how hard I tried, my eyes kept straying to his lips. Their subtle provocative movements, the way they parted and formed each word, consumed me with curiosity. Dare I admit it? I wanted him to kiss me again.

"You must understand, Miss Barlow. This house is not equipped for boarders," he explained. "I apologize for not being able to accommodate you but I think it would be best—for both of us—if you secured lodgings elsewhere. I would be happy to place some calls on your behalf if you'd like."

Good sense told me it was for the best, that I should leave and find a nice comfortable inn somewhere, but there was just one thing stopping me, one tiny inconsequential thing—I didn't want to go. "No."

My reluctance to leave this entombment of a house was just as great a shock to me as it was to Lord Boothe. His brow raised in question at my refusal to leave. "No? Are you rejecting my help or my request to leave, Miss Barlow?"

"I don't think anyone is going anywhere." A man with sand colored hair, warm brown eyes and a lop-sided grin stepped into the room. "There'll be no traveling on that road for awhile," he added. Though he appeared to have just come from the rains outside, tousled wet hair and rumpled overcoat shedding their raindrops to the floor, he seemed to be in a jovial mood, and when he turned to me I found his smile infectious.

"Hello," he greeted me. "Graham Ferguson at your service." With great gallantry he lifted my hand to his lips and bestowed a kiss on it. "And you are?"

"Meredith Barlow," I replied, flattered by the attention.

"Miss Barlow, of course! I'm glad to see you made it safe and sound."

"Graham!" Lord Boothe interrupted. "You're dripping on the floor!"

The other man looked down at the sodden carpet. "Oh right. Don't go away." And with a wink he was gone.

Confused, I looked to my host for some insight.

"Graham is another resident here Miss Barlow." Contempt burned in his eyes for the other man. "He managed Boothe House in my absence until recently. He is, among other things, my cousin."

"A fact you hate to admit, eh Eric?" Graham rejoined us. He seemed not the least bit disturbed by his cousin's animosity toward him. In fact, he took it all in with a chuckle.

The two men were a contrasting pair; where Lord Boothe was darkly attractive, Graham, with his sun-dappled hair and doe-like eyes, possessed an engaging appearance.

He made himself at home at the table. "It was my fault for the misunderstanding about your lease. As you've noticed, I'm sure, Boothe House needs a few repairs."

I smiled sympathetically. "A little redecorating wouldn't hurt."

He laughed. "Yes, that too. It all adds up, you know. I had heard of a few estates opening up to the public and I thought, what a grand idea! I assumed I had authority in such matters, but you set me straight on that score, didn't you, Eric?"

Lord Boothe didn't answer. He just leaned casually back in his chair with his chin resting in his hand, the creased frown on his face I had had the displeasure of seeing before.

"So here you are," Graham commented to me, "and it looks like here you'll stay. Luck has shined upon us, or should I say rained upon us." He laughed at his own cleverness. "I don't think even cousin Eric would force such a charming creature like yourself to walk back to the village in these horrid conditions."

Graham baited his cousin like a child with a sugar treat who refused to share. Lord Boothe tossed the napkin from his lap onto the table as he stood. "Of course you are welcome to stay Miss Barlow, for as long as is *necessary*."

"Thank you," I murmured, somewhat elated, yet disappointed in knowing that my definition of necessary was vastly different from his.

"If you'll excuse me." He bowed his head before leaving.

My eyes followed his retreating back. Even when quitting a room the man commanded attention. Oh, how I loathed him.

"Well, I for one am delighted that you're staying," Graham interjected. "Maybe you can breathe a little life into the old place."

"I don't think the rest of the household shares your sentiment."

He shrugged. "Eric is always in a sour mood for one reason or another. I wouldn't take it to heart."

"I'm afraid this time I am the reason," I confessed. "When I arrived last night he mistook me for someone else and was quite upset when he realized I wasn't that someone."

Realization dawned on Graham's face. "Ah, Paulette!"

"Paulette. Yes." Rancor seeped into my voice unexpectedly.

"That's what I say. A bit of a snob, that one." He looked about to see if we were being overheard then edged closer to whisper, "She was Eric's Paris diversion. The last I heard, she had left him for a banker. He was quite put out, of course. What a kick in the teeth that must have been to find out she beat him to the cut," he mused. "It was just a matter of time. Eric has quite a jealous streak, another trait of the Boothe curse."

"The curse?" First a haunting; then a curse? For a cold, dreary house it was becoming quite colorful.

"Surely you've heard of the infamous Boothe curse where all the men in the family fall victim to insanity?"

"Only the men?" I asked.

"We're a very selective family."

"You seem quite normal."

"Just wait until there's a full moon." He gave a little howl for effect.

I liked Graham. He made me laugh and feel human again. He didn't seem to be affected by the discord that was so prevalent in the house. I imagined him having a rather rambunctious childhood. He had a spirit and sense of humor I admired.

"Then I suppose you're on personal terms with the ghost in the east wing," I teased.

"Of course, but we can't leave out my chess partner in the west wing."

"So the house is haunted?"

"I hate to disappoint you but, no. It's just more superstitious drivel the villagers conjured up to amuse themselves."

"I didn't really believe your cousin anyway."

"Eric?" he asked in disbelief.

I nodded. "He hinted that spirits from beyond roamed the halls."

He shrugged. "I'm surprised he even mentioned it. It's always been a sore spot with him." He dismissed the notion with a wave of his hand. "Ah well, all this ghoulish talk has made me famished. Linnea?"

"I wouldn't bother her, if I were you. She made sure my breakfast was ice cold because I was late. I shudder to think what she'll serve you at this late hour."

"That's Linnea for you. She was just letting you know who's boss in the kitchen. You have to know how to handle her." With a wink and the smile that ingratiated me to him he called again for the cook, but in his own style. "Linnea darling, you know I can not start my day without seeing those glorious dimples of yours."

Almost immediately the door swung open and Linnea bustled in, beaming, dimples and all; and in her hand, a plate piled with steaming sausages, ham and eggs. I doubted the flattery would have the same effect coming from me.

I met the housekeeper, Ana, back in my room in a flurry of mops and beeswax. She was a prim, squat little woman with a piggish snout that she constantly wiped at with the back of her hand. She snorted and wheezed her way through her task of clearing the room of the many layers of dust, making me wonder why she would take a position that was such an irritant to her physical well-being. The enormous house was a massive undertaking for a staff of five, much less one. I understood now why the majority of the rooms were left to fester. When she began a fit of sneezes I offered to complete the dusting.

"Oh no, Miss," she said, "It's Lord Boothe's orders that I make this room fit."

Lord Boothe? I was shocked yet duly impressed. "Were you the one who left the room open last night?" I wondered.

She shook her head vehemently. "No, this room is usually off limits to the staff."

"Then who ...?"

"I'd not be knowing that," she replied in a tone that bespoke her unwillingness to meddle in the affairs of her employer.

My question had still to be answered. The melodious chime of the mantel clock drew my attention reminding me of yet another unanswered question.

The small gold clock sat unimposing between the cherub statuettes, but I couldn't help being drawn by it. The delicate filigreed hands were set against a backdrop of ivory white. It was ten o'clock and according to my watch the correct time. Who had kept the timepiece running in a supposedly forbidden room? Graham perhaps? Had he opened the room knowing of my impending arrival? Or was it Lord Boothe? Was this room a secret sanctuary of sorts? The man impressed me as having many hidden facets. But for whatever reason, I was here and gladly so.

With Ana's last swipe of the cloth the wood gleamed to reflection. When she began unpacking the leather case I had left in the car I wondered if the case had miraculously grown feet.

"That was master Graham's doing," she informed me. "He brought the things up just after you went down to breakfast."

My typewriter and writing supplies were all neatly arranged on the writing desk. I smiled at Graham's thoughtfulness. I then wondered how Lucille fared overnight. She was a dear and faithful friend and I hated to leave her in such dire circumstances, but I promised to make it up to her with a good wash and polish.

Ana continued unpacking my suitcase, hanging my day clothes in the armoire and my more personal attire in the dressing room. I couldn't permit myself to sit idly by while I watched someone else do a chore I was perfectly capable of doing. I explained to the little housekeeper that I preferred to handle my own things, and she was free to move on to her other duties. She protested at first, but I sensed her relief.

Halfway through, I realized I was unpacking several weeks worth of clothes for a mere few day's stay. It was ridiculous, of course, so I removed all but what I needed from the bureau and replaced them in my case. A powder blue handkerchief caught my eye. It was lying there with my things, probably picked up when I was repacking. The elegant pink monogram of *MB* declared it mine, but I did not recognize it. I went back to the bureau, now very curious, and searched the drawer. Its mate sat neatly folded in a crest shape under the paper liner. It still held a faint trace of the sweet ginger perfume from the bottle on the dressing table. The handkerchiefs were returned to their rightful place.

I was curious about the woman to whom they belonged. Was she happy living in Boothe House? In this room? I looked about at the curtains, the perfume bottles, the pen on the writing desk—the things she had touched. She decorated the room with the things she loved best: leafy green images of endless life. Her most treasured possession was the mantel clock, though how I knew this I was not sure; it was just a feeling, an instinct.

She sat at the writing desk often as I was doing; looking out over a sun-drenched garden that was now a soaked, gnarling tangle of weeds. How sad she would be to see it now. The sullen sky dampened my own mood.

I looked down at my writing tablet and endless supply of pens and pencils. All was in readiness for the creativity to flow. I had wasted enough time already. Feeling there was no better time than the present, I dove into my work. The unanswered question remained: When a woman is alone among strangers, whom does she trust? I scribed a few pages then crumpled them up in disgust. I began again only to toss the lifeless sheets into the wastebasket with the others. My words lacked substance and heart. My mind kept wandering back to the kiss. I needed passion. Yes, that was it, a story of heartfelt love against the backdrop of a mystery. It sounded promising. Now, if I could only write it.

Inspiration came slowly. The farthest I wrote was a brief description of the hero: tall, handsome, a mysteriously brooding man with raven hair and perceptive grey eyes that denounced every effort of my being.

"Lord of Mercy!" I exclaimed. I had just described Lord Boothe. The paper sailed neatly into the wastebasket. Where was my mind? On his kiss. One kiss does not a hero make. I would do better to concentrate on my heroine.

She would like a room such as this, full of color and life. She may even wear a perfume of sweetened ginger spice. Just who was the woman who lived here? She seemed to be everywhere in this room, yet I hadn't a clue. Inspiration was coming. Maybe if I knew a little bit more about her ...

Answers would not be found sitting idly by, so I ventured down to the library. If neither Lord Boothe nor Graham were present, a family record may be shelved there—maybe a bible or tree chart. The room was empty, but I assumed it was a temporary situation for this was the only room where a fire had been lit.

I helped myself to a lamp on the mantel and lit it with a burning switch from the fire. As I carefully replaced the glass chimney the flame rose illuminating the portrait over the fireplace. I raised the lamp to scan the entire picture. I don't know why I hadn't noticed it before. I guess I presumed it was a man, the old lord perhaps. But it wasn't. It was of a woman. Her raven colored hair was swept off her ageless cream-like face. Her smile was serene, but her dewy blue eyes held sadness. The mistress of my garden room. I knew it instantly in my heart. But she seemed very familiar ...

My breath caught in my throat when I remembered where I had seen her before. It was in my dream. She was the woman who invaded my dream making her sadness my own. I rubbed at my arms suddenly feeling chilled as if I had just passed a forbidden barrier.

Lord Boothe entered and stood quietly behind me gazing up at the portrait upon which I was so transfixed. "Who is she?" I asked.

"That," he replied in a less than affectionate tone, "is Madelaine Boothe.

Madelaine Boothe? *MB*, like on the handkerchiefs in the bureau drawer. There she was so obviously before me. I turned around with so many questions running through my mind. I stopped, though, as I took in his glassy stare. The mistress of my garden room was not as revered as I imagined her to be. She was some villainess from a tormenting chapter of his life. His eyes, pained and angry, swept down the portrait to my own. His voice became hard with malice. "She was my mother."

≈ FOUR ≈

How anyone could hold such contempt for the woman who nurtured and gave birth to him posed a sacrilege to me. I had lost my own mother at the tender age of ten. The memories of her would always live on in my heart.

"Were you very young when she died?" I asked.

His grim set lips widened in a sardonic smile. "I was old enough. Old enough to realize that a mother's affections could easily be swayed."

The dream became quite vivid in my mind. What had happened to the little boy who looked upon his mother with adoration in his eyes? The little boy was still there deep within him; only now, a mask of hatred and hurt cloaked the child. "She may not have shown it but surely your mother loved you," I contended. In fact, I was certain of it.

"My relationship with my mother was not a natural one. Just as love is, contempt can also be a mutual affection." Disapproval must have shown on my face. "That wasn't the answer you were expecting, was it? My dear Miss Barlow, life does not imitate those fanciful stories you create. We don't all see candied apples and orange blossoms. Life can be hard with little pleasure."

His patronizing set my defenses up. "I'm very well aware of the misfortunes life can bring, sir. My stories are not meant to be a recreation of life but an escape from it. Some people like to leave all their miseries behind for a time and read something that makes them smile."

"I apologize, Miss Barlow, if I offended you. I didn't mean to imply that your stories were unworthy of reading."

"Didn't you?"

He didn't answer. Instead, his lips turned up in challenge.

"Have you read any of my stories?" I asked him, a smile on my own lips.

"No," he admitted. "I have not had the pleasure."

"Then maybe you should reserve your judgment until you have."

He acquiesced with a nod. "Touché Miss Barlow. Or may I call you Meredith? After our rather intimate introduction last night I think we can dispense with the formalities."

What slight victory I may have celebrated was instantly extinguished. The topic of our kiss was one I preferred to avoid, and he knew it. I had hoped to be spared further humiliation, but if I had learned one thing about Lord Boothe it was that he spared no one.

"I'm sorry Meredith," he said. "I'm making you uncomfortable aren't I?"

I was "Meredith" now. "No. Not in the least." My fingers fumbled with a stray thread from my pocket.

"I do apologize again for my rather forward behavior last night. If you had said something or stopped me ..."

And I hadn't, had I? If I recalled correctly, I wasn't the only one with delayed reflexes. Two could play at that game. "Really—Eric, it's nothing to concern yourself with. Don't think any more of it." I smiled. Then to set him back a bit I lied. "God knows I haven't."

His injured ego paused to recover. A show of respect broadened his lips. "Good!" He held out his hand in offering. "Truce?"

I accepted it. "Truce." But I still loathed him.

Now that we had steered away from the distressing topic of his childhood the lines in his face softened. The wall of arrogance he wore like a heavy cologne seemed to dissolve. He moved behind the desk, removed a book from it and placed it on the bookshelf.

"So tell me Meredith, what brings a nice young woman like yourself out to this remote part of the country?"

"I wasn't having much success in starting my latest book, so I decided to change my setting."

"And has it helped?"

"Not yet."

He studied me. "Boothe House wasn't at all what you were expecting was it?"

"To be honest—no," I replied.

"I thought not. Graham was right; the place does need extensive work. Unfortunately the rents aren't enough to cover it."

"You could always raise the rents—or take in boarders," I suggested.

He smiled at my obvious attempt to settle our disagreement. "I can't ask the villagers to pay more rent on the land than they can afford; and as for boarders ... let's just say that I prefer to keep my personal affairs private. That's why I'm selling it."

"But hasn't the house been in your family for generations?"

He nodded. "And it might stay that way if I can't find a buyer who isn't squeamish. Would you buy a house if you were led to believe that it was haunted or possessed by demons?"

The idea did have merit for curiosity's sake, but I doubted I would spend any significant amount on something so questionable. "No," I answered. "I don't think I would."

"You're not alone. I've had three prospective buyers in the past three months. The last one backed down yesterday. It seems his accountants advised against investing in such an unstable venture. What I don't understand is how they found out about that ridiculous rumor."

"I seem to recall someone inferring just such a rumor to me last night," I posed.

His smile turned impish. "It was a low tactic, I admit, but I can assure you that there is no truth in it."

"That's a shame," I said. "I was hoping to find a new chess partner."

A burst of energy blew into the room startling us both. "There you are!" Graham called. "I was looking for you. I thought you might like a tour of the place. Hello, Eric! Boring our guest again?"

"No, Graham, I leave that to you," Eric rejoined.

"Oh come now, don't be modest; you're the expert. I'm much better at entertaining. Shall we?"

I took his offered arm. "Yes, thank you." Turning to Eric, I asked, "Aren't you going to join us?"

"He's already seen the place," Graham answered. "Besides, I'm sure he has more important things to do. You know how taxing paperwork is for those barrister types."

We left the lord of the manor with a sinister frown on his face.

"Is your cousin really a barrister?" I inquired. That would explain the browbeating.

"Yes. Eric followed in his father's footsteps like a dutiful lad. His practice is in London."

"And you didn't follow?"

"No, I chose medicine instead."

"So you're a doctor?" I said duly impressed.

"No." There was an edge of regret in his answer. "I never finished. When Uncle Edmund became ill I left to take care of the place. I've sort of dedicated my life to it now."

"You could always go back to medical school."

He shrugged. "Who knows? I just might."

We started with the main floor; the sitting room where seldom seen visitors were received, the smoking room or drawing room as they preferred it, the formal and informal dining rooms, and the kitchen.

Linnea was busy preparing the evening meal and showed, with pursed lips and furrowed brow, her displeasure at being interrupted. Graham, with his fawning flattery, soon brought out the dimples I was hard pressed to believe the woman even possessed.

She opened a pot for Graham's inspection, releasing the aroma of steaming sweet smells. He proclaimed her creation a work of art. I leaned over to sample the aroma myself only to have the lid slammed shut in my face.

I then had the audacity to peek under a cloth at the rising bread on the center table. My reward was a stinging slap to the hand with a wooden spoon.

Graham found her behavior quite amusing. I was not amused at all. She was looking for some form of entertainment and found it in me. Did she behave like this with all their guests or was I the chosen one?

Graham chuckled. "Consider yourself lucky. She usually just ignores people. She must like you."

There was little comfort in that.

As we moved through the house, down dimly lit corridors to vacant musty rooms, I was aware of Graham's affection for the old place. His eyes caressed every room with warmth and tenderness. I found it hard to imagine anyone finding the cold, deteriorating place a comforting home, but Graham had lived there most of his life, and saw beyond the decay to what the place had once been.

I tried to look at each room through Graham's eyes—the magnificence of the architecture, the fine styles of Victorian and Georgian periods—but I still felt like a trespasser, unwanted and scorned.

With Graham's easy wit and charm I enjoyed myself regardless of the gloomy surroundings. "And up here we have the bedrooms," he remarked as we stepped onto the second floor landing. "The hall to the right is reserved for our most distinguished guests like yourself. The Duke of Marlborough himself stayed here on numerous occasions back when my grandfather lived here. Of course we haven't entertained in years. Most of the rooms have been left to rot, I'm afraid. Over here," he led me to the left, "is where the family resides. Eric's room is down on the right, and this is my room. Care to have a look?" Graham added with a devilish gleam.

"Oh, no," I replied. "I think I prefer the safety of the hall."

"Don't you trust me?" he asked, wounded.

"Not in the least."

He narrowed his eyes then laughed aloud. "Hah! Smart girl. I like you. We must do something to keep you around for awhile."

"Why? So you can break down my resistance with your sweet words and flattery, hoping to lure me into a tryst?"

"It has a nice ring to it, doesn't it?"

"Hmm. You could get into a great deal of trouble flirting like that"

Graham's smile turned wicked. "One can only hope, dear lady. One can only hope." His eyebrows jumped mischievously.

I felt giddy and lighthearted. I found myself caught up in the harmless flirtation, and I liked it. "I see I will have to remain on my toes around you."

"And so you shall. Come. The dance floor beckons you." He bowed and swept a gallant hand toward the third floor staircase.

"The dance floor?"

With a tawny-eyed wink he added, "I was saving the best for last. The entire third floor is a Boothe House original. A ballroom complete with its own orchestra. You don't believe me. Tsk, tsk." He shook his head. "Such a doubting Thomas. Come and see for yourself."

I went along with the game though I was skeptical. I did not think he had any dubious intentions in mind, but one had to question what he was up to; a ballroom complete with orchestra was hard to believe.

He bade me to close my eyes and took my hand to lead me the rest of the way. I heard the click of a doorknob and the creak of ancient hinges. He left me there attuned to every sound. His footsteps proceeded forward for some distance. "No peeking."

His voice echoed through the air in what must be a very spacious room, I surmised.

He continued moving through the room, my head turning, following his direction. My anticipation grew. What sort of room was this? I kept my promise and held my eyes tightly shut. "Where are we? The attic?"

He laughed but did not answer. My sense of smell became acutely aware of a burning scent, the acrid smell of something old and dirty, covered with mildew being put to flame. I became alarmed.

Without making a sound he crept up beside me and whispered softly in my ear, "Open your eyes."

I opened them slowly, unsure of what I would find. My mouth gaped in awe at the splendor before me. Music began, a waltz played by a small music box, the sound bringing the room to life. The gentlemen and ladies muraled on the walls seemed to sway and dance as the lamps flickered above them. In the center of the room, high above, hung a chandelier, its now dull crystals reflecting only half its beauty in the pale glow. But the most magnificent part of the room was the windows. They reached from floor to ceiling on each side of the room exposing a breathtaking view of the valley.

"May I have this dance?"

My chin hung in astonishment.

"And you didn't believe me. Now do you trust me?" he asked.

"Implicitly!" I replied as he swept me onto the floor.

We continued the tour in grand style, swirling to every corner "Over here," he said, steering me swiftly to the windows, "is a view of the entire estate. The old barn there to the right is now a garage. A new barn was built down by the lake, there, just beyond those trees. They're both in sad shape, I'm afraid. The old nags don't seem to mind though."

"Which? Horses or motorcars?"

"Both." He laughed.

"What is that down there attached to the house?" I asked.

"A greenhouse."

"Can we see it?" The tranquility and lushness of a green house always appealed to me.

"There's nothing to see. It hasn't been used in years. Now over here you may find something of interest." The music carried us to yet another part of the room. Graham held the door open for me to peek in. "This is the kitchen complete with china, linens, banquet tables, stove, icebox and my personal favorite, the dumb waiter. Eric and I used to ride up the thing when we were children and scare the life out of the servants."

"Where does it lead?"

"To the kitchen and then down to the wine cellar. Care to have a ride?"

The offer was tempting, but I felt ridiculous even contemplating the idea. What was it about Graham that made me feel so reckless and irresponsible in his presence? Traits I sensed he never grew out of? I shook my head. "Another time, perhaps."

"I'll hold you to it."

He was a wonderful, agile dancer. I felt light and graceful under his expert lead. "Where did you learn to dance so well? Is your cousin as skilled as you?" Would it matter if he weren't? Somehow I knew that if Eric held a woman in the whisper closeness of a dance she wouldn't care how graceful he was.

"Aunt Madelaine insisted that we were instructed in all the social graces. We were never allowed to put them to the test of course; young boys were too much of a nuisance to have at parties. But Eric and I would sneak up into the kitchen over there through the dumb waiter to watch all the guests and steal a treat or two."

"Did they entertain often?"

"No, not like my grandfather did. There was a tradition of a masquerade right around this time of year. Uncle Edmund kept it up until Aunt Madelaine left us. He didn't have the heart to keep it up after that."

Our dance slowed to a gentle sway. "Do you miss her?"

"Aunt Madelaine?" he asked aghast. "No, not in the least. She was a very selfish and foolish woman. Oh, she made the effort of trying to be the mother I never had, but her heart was never in it. She had eyes only for Eric. He was her pride and joy until she tired of him and moved on to someone else."

"Was he very upset when she died?"

The dance stopped abruptly. "Who told you she died?" he asked with alarm.

"Eric did."

"Then he must know something I don't. The last we saw of Aunt Madelaine was just before she ran away with one of her lovers. I believe I was nine at the time. Eric was seven."

I stood motionless trying to digest the news. "Then why did Eric say she died?"

He sighed, "I don't know. I've learned never to question Eric's reasoning. The answers will leave you more confused than before. Maybe she did die since that time. Who knows? Good riddance is what I say. She was certainly deserving of it."

"That's rather callous don't you think?" I remarked.

"She was a callous woman," he defended. He glanced at his watch. "Look at the time. I think we better end our tour here. It's almost time for supper. You know how Linnea hates to be kept waiting."

"Yes, I know all too well. Aren't you coming?"

"I have to close the room back up. You run ahead. Do you think you can find your way?"

"I think so," I assured him, though I was not so assured myself. "Thank you for the dance."

"It was my pleasure," he said warmly, the smile back on his face. "Now hurry along, I don't want to be the cause of your indigestion."

Why was he so impatient to be rid of me? He seemed to be in a hurry all of a sudden and I knew it was not because he wanted to be on time for supper. Linnea would wait for him till the ends of time. No, he was up to something, and I was curious to see what.

Pretending to leave, I turned back and hid behind the door. Graham removed a lamp from the wall and walked into the kitchen. I followed keeping my footsteps as silent as possible. At the door I stopped and pressed my ear to listen. There was movement within and the sound of a rusty pulley squeaking as it turned. The dumb waiter? I opened the door to see the light from his lamp fade down the hole in the wall. What was down there that couldn't wait? I sighed. Some boys never grew up.

Having been temporarily lost in the maze of hallways, I entered my room at quarter to the hour. I quickly stepped out of my clothes and into a burgundy off-the-shoulder evening gown. Dinner would be formal, I assumed, so I chose my best gown for the occasion. It was long and elegant, a trifle too formal for a dinner for three, but the gown suited me well and I did so want to make an impression.

I sat at the dressing table and glanced over at the forgotten writing desk where my tablet and pen rested unmoved. And that was where they would stay for yet another day. The plot unfolding in Boothe House was much too intriguing to ignore.

Something terrible must have happened to the loving little boy that Eric once was to cause him to grow into such an angry, bitter man. I refused to believe that Madelaine Boothe was as wicked as they would have me believe. My instincts told me there was more to the story.

I finished with my hair and took stock of my appearance. What I saw pleased me, yet I was puzzled. The gown was beautiful, and the burgundy enhanced my color; however, the reflection I saw was not my own but another woman's—Madelaine's.

❧ FIVE ❧

Her sorrowful blue eyes stared back at me. From the crown of her ebony hair to the peach satin of her bodice, her appearance slowly filled in my reflection. Too frightened to scream and too curious to move, I sat motionless, aware of each beat of my anxious heart.

White ginger. The scent was soft and sweet. It wasn't just a trick of light; I could smell her perfume, too. Her skin was perfectly smooth and nearly translucent; her mouth void of a smile. But it was something in her eyes that caught my breath and let time stand still. In them I saw a legion of unshed tears and desperation—a lonely soul yearning to be healed.

I had seen that look of despair somewhere before—

"Miss?"

The sharp knock on the door sent me to my feet. The bench seat toppled behind me. For being such a small woman, Ana had the knuckles of a bear.

"Yes?" I called. My hand pressed against my chest, my palm absorbing the shock to my heart.

"The master is waiting for you in the dining room," she replied.

The lady in the mirror pressed a finger to her lips.

"I ... I'll be right there."

When I looked back, she was gone. The scent of ginger faded to a brief memory. From my heart to the mirror, I reached out to touch the place of her image. The glass felt cool and solid against my fingertips. It was more than I could say for my current emotional state.

Recollection of another vision haunted my memory. I was ten. It happened only days after my mother had died. Every night for a week I saw her sitting in the chair by my bed just as she used to do, a book in her lap, spectacles perched on the bridge of her nose. She read *Alice in Wonderland*, by Lewis Carroll while I lay snug under the covers drifting off to sleep. I even felt her warm lips against my cheek.

Good night. Sweet dreams. Sleep tight.

I was so sure her death was all just a mistake. The Colonel had been less than enthusiastic about my discovery. With tears in his eyes he explained to me that my desire to see her again was so strong I actually believed I did. It was just my imagination, he said. My mother was never coming back. That night he took away the chair from my room. I never saw her again.

Through the years I had pushed the episode to the back of my mind. Now the memory came flooding back and with it uncertainty. Could my strong desire to meet Madelaine overpower my sense of reality?

I was no longer a child. I knew the difference between fiction and nonfiction. What I saw was real. My sanity required proof, however.

But how does one prove they've seen a ghost?

Eric stood at the sideboard pouring himself a glass of sherry. He wore the black suit jacket and starched white shirt with precision as if they were specifically tailored for a man who liked the feel of fine clothes close to his skin.

"Sorry, I'm late," I said, my steps faltering only slightly in my haste.

He turned. My lips quivered in an attempt to smile. I wanted him to see me as something more than a nuisance, to admire my expensive dress and look at me with appreciation in his eyes.

Instead, he set down his glass and rushed to my side, a deep furrow of concern creasing his brow.

"What's wrong?" He asked reaching for my hand. "Has something happened?"

"Nothing's wrong," I assured him. And as to what happened, I didn't want to elaborate on it at the moment. The last thing I needed was Eric concluding I suffered from hallucinatory episodes. "I'm fine."

"No you're not. Your face is pale and your hands □ they're ice cold. Here." He grabbed the glass of sherry off the sideboard and slipped it into my hands. "Drink this," he ordered.

I surveyed the sherry skeptically. Alcohol no matter how slight made me do silly things. Now more than ever, I needed my wits about me.

"It will put some color back into your cheeks," he coaxed.

There was no arguing that point. I could always use a little extra color. I took a tentative sip then a healthy gulp. The sherry tasted sweet and felt smooth sliding down my throat warming me from the inside out.

"One more," Eric prescribed.

I looked up into his hard features hovering protectively close to mine. I remembered, now, where I had seen that look on Madelaine's face before. In Eric. Inwardly, his spirit grieved. I had the uncanny desire to reach out and ease the lonely desperation I saw there just as I had wanted to do for Madelaine.

I knew then that I had too much of the sherry. I set the glass down before I was tempted to empty it. "I'm fine," I repeated, still feeling awkward under his scrutiny.

He placed his hand on the arm of the chair and leaned mere inches from my face. I felt his sigh against my lips. "You're not fine, Meredith."

It was the way he breathed my name that subdued my defenses. Like an embrace it solicited trust.

"You're trembling," he said. "Something is obviously troubling you, now what is it?"

What was troubling me? My mind grappled with what I thought to be real; my skin vibrated with every sound I heard and every movement of air I felt; and my heart raced to quell the lack of judgement I feared taking hold of my senses. What was troubling me? It would be easier to ask what wasn't.

"If someone has done something to upset you, I hope you have the good sense to confide in me," he said.

"And if it's you," I queried.

He laughed as he stood. "Past experience tells me you wouldn't hesitate to point out my faults—no matter how much I protested."

He was right. I would relish the opportunity. But his faults weren't in question, mine were. "My only trouble is being coddled like a baby," I said, hoping to end the discussion. "I've always been short-winded. I may not be used to climbing up and down so many stairs but I think I'll recover. I'm a big girl."

He poured himself a sherry and rose it to a toast. "So I've noticed."

As he took a swig of the sweetened wine, my second sip finally kicked in. A rush of heat spread up to the roots of my hair. So he had noticed, after all.

"Your color seems to be coming back," he noted with a wolfish grin.

The man truly had no scruples. It was just like the wretch to notice. "Does that mean I'm cured, Doctor?"

He finished the glass in one swallow. "I'd say you're out of danger. Unless you feel you need more reviving."

"A master of resuscitation, are you?" I teased.

"When the need arises," he murmured. Alone, his smile was charming; coupled with candlelight and a few drops of sherry it was completely disarming.

Linnea burst through the door, a soup bowl in each hand. I was delighted for the interruption. She set the bowls down at each place then dipped a quick curtsy before heading back into the kitchen.

"Shall we?" Eric invited.

"Shouldn't we wait for Graham?" I wondered, hoped.

"No," he replied assisting me with my chair. "Waiting for Graham will only lead to cold food and indigestion. Please begin."

I couldn't help but notice that I sat in the chair directly to the left of Eric, far from my previous seat at the foot of the table and intimately close to the head. I began the conversation with a mundane comment on the weather. I didn't trust myself with anything more scintillating, not with the sherry still dancing through my veins. Then I remembered how my existence at Boothe House hinged on the very topic. "Graham said the rain is likely to last until the weekend," I noted.

Eric scoffed. "I wouldn't put too much stock into Graham's forecasts. His expertise lies mostly in the past not the future."

"Why don't you like Graham?" There, I'd said it. The question had been rambling around in my head since I first came and now it was out in the open.

Eric laid down his spoon and regarded me with a sidelong glance. "I don't dislike my cousin, Miss Barlow."

We were back to "Miss Barlow" again. I must have hit a nerve. "Then why are the two of you constantly bickering?"

"Bickering?" He chuckled. "Miss Barlow, you have to understand that although we were raised as brothers, Graham and I have separate interests. Our "bickering", as you so call it, is only a reflection of that. Rest assured that I have only the best interests in his welfare."

Eric Boothe was a terrible liar. The animosity I witnessed between them ran deeper than separate interests did. Graham's timely entrance only proved my point.

I watched as Eric's countenance began to fade and his jaw tighten.

"Sorry I'm late." Graham stopped first at my chair to kiss my hand. "Meredith, you are a vision."

"Thank you," I replied mildly flattered. Graham's approval

was important to me, of course, but I knew he would give it regardless of his true feelings. Graham was only too eager to please, unlike Eric, who would only give his approval if he felt it was deserved.

Graham took his seat. "Did I miss anything?"

"Just supper as usual," Eric commented dryly. He tossed his napkin aside, rested his elbows on the arms of the chair and steepled his fingers.

"It couldn't be helped, old man. I had to lock up the ballroom."

Eric sat up straight. "The ballroom? What were you doing up there?"

"It was my fault," I interjected. "Graham was kind enough to show it to me. I'm afraid I got carried away with all my questions. It's a remarkable room. Have you ever thought about opening it up again?"

"There's no reason to," Eric said. "We don't have extravagant balls anymore."

"Maybe you should," I suggested.

"A party?" Graham elated. "I like the sound of that."

Eric shook his head, prepared to dismiss the idea entirely. "The house isn't in any condition to host a party."

"I'm sure with a good cleaning it could be presentable," I reasoned. "You could invite all those skittish buyers you've been wooing. They could see for themselves what a valuable investment Boothe House is and perhaps make an offer you can't refuse."

The idea of unloading the house seemed to strike a cord. Once more, I had Eric's undivided attention.

Graham shook his head. "Maybe it's not such a good idea after all. It would take a goodly sum just for the repairs not too mention all the food, extra servants ..."

Eric interrupted, "It may not be plausible, but any idea is worth considering. I'll look into it. If it will help sell this tomb I'm all for it."

After supper we retired to the library. Graham brought out a deck of cards and some match sticks and proceeded to teach me the intricacies of poker.

Eric, quiet and sullen, took his place behind his desk with the excuse of overdue paperwork. His dinner jacket was slung over the back of the chair and his sleeves were rolled to his elbows ready for work. He pondered over books and ledgers while, Graham and I, sat on the rug with our cards and matchsticks. He sat working by oil lamp, listening to our camaraderie yet remaining distant. Whenever Graham was present Eric seemed to withdraw into himself. I wondered just what had transpired between the two men to keep them at constant odds. They had been raised together, but were no closer than mortal enemies. Whatever had happened, no chisel or hammer could remove the wedge between them.

With a winner's pot heaped with matchsticks, I laid down the winning hand and claimed the booty. Graham was dismayed but would not be bested. He declared the next round his game of choice.

"Truth or consequences," he decided. "I'll ask you a question and you either have to answer it truthfully or pay the consequences."

Something told me I was headed for disaster. "I don't know. This game sounds dangerous. What do you think, Eric? Should I have my counsel present?"

He lifted his gaze off the papers stacked on the desk and cocked his head. "Are you asking me to represent you?"

"And if I am?" I studied his face and noted a slight lift at the corners of his lips.

"If it was anything but a game I would lay my defenses at your disposal, but in this case I think you can handle yourself. I've seen you in action. Graham hasn't a chance."

"Eric won't play a game if he thinks he's going to lose," Graham replied hotly.

"Very well, I'll go first," I said, hoping to prevent a war from breaking out among the ranks. "Graham, if you could be any animal in the world, what would you be?"

"Hmm." Graham tapped his fingers against his chin. "I know. How about a wolf?"

Eric covered his snicker with a cough. "How fitting," he mumbled.

"Don't pay any attention to him," I instructed Graham. "He has no imagination. Now what about a wolf."

"Well, I was just thinking how fierce and loyal a wolf is and—yes, a wolf would suit me perfectly."

"Fair enough. Now it's your turn." I braced my back against the leg of a chair and tucked my legs underneath me. "Give it your best shot," I told him.

Graham rubbed his hands together taking steady aim, then smiled. "When was your most memorable kiss?"

Bull's eye. He couldn't have picked a more sensitive subject if he tried. I had been kissed on more than one occasion during my youth and adolescence, but the only kiss I could remember with any clarity was the one that happened right there in that very room.

"Don't keep us in suspense," Eric said with more than a hint of curiosity. He knew precisely what my answer would be because he was the one who had left the most memorable impression on my lips.

"I thought you weren't playing," I snapped in his direction.

"I wasn't☐until now."

I couldn't answer truthfully; nor could I lie. "I'll take the consequences."

"Coward," Eric taunted.

Better a coward than a blithering fool. "So what will it be?" I turned to Graham. "I'm at your mercy." With swatches of honey-colored hair falling over his brow and a grin the size of Big Ben, he looked almost child-like. "Shall I hold a spoon up by my nose? Or would you prefer a pencil?"

"Actually," he drawled. "I was thinking more on the lines of a recital."

A recital? I cringed. I was a writer not a speaker.

"Of one of your stories," Graham continued. "And I know just which one." He jumped to his feet and scanned the many shelves of books. Not finding what he sought he bolted for the door. "I must have left it upstairs. Don't move."

"I wouldn't dream of it." As if I could. Blood had already left my legs and I could feel them drifting off to sleep.

"So what possesses a single young woman to take on the profession of writing?" Eric inquired.

A hint of skepticism edged his query, but the fact that he addressed my writing as a career instead of a hobby impressed me enough to answer truthfully. Writing had always been a part of my life. I lived and breathed the lyrical word. "I can't remember a time when I wasn't thinking up stories," I answered. "Whenever I was frightened of a storm or the dark, my mother would help me create my own fairy tales to help me get through the night. I guess I never stopped."

It was something he would probably never understand, especially coming from a woman. I ran into men's dismissal of women's literature often enough to know that they seldom changed their views on the subject. It would be a difficult task to sway his way of thinking—a challenge I looked forward to conquering.

Graham returned and placed *Chamber Secrets* in my hands. It was a compilation of short romantic mysteries and one of my first books. My fingers traced over the gold embossed lettering on the cover. It looked brand new. That fact that Graham went out of his way to procure a copy of my work touched me deeply.

"*The Green Room*, please," he bade as he adjusted himself on the floor against a row of pillow cushions.

Beginning on page one, I read by firelight, speaking soft and evenly. "If I could grant you one wish, what would it be? Lady Sophia asked the prisoner ..."

The Green Room was nearly half over when I heard the soft rumble of a snore. Graham reclined on the pillows in a contented sleep—not quite the response I was hoping for. With a sigh, I quietly closed the book.

"Don't stop." The plea startled me. Eric sat by the desk, his arm crooked at the elbow, his temple resting against his palm and his long legs stretched out in front of him in repose. "Please."

Reopening the book, I began where I had left off. The crack and squeak of my sudden shyness sounded out of tune in the stillness of the room. I forced my throat to relax and read the passages as I had written them—with my heart. I glanced up now and again to see if I had put Eric to sleep as well, but he sat listening intently to my every word.

The story proclaimed a hero's courage in conquering his foes and the passion he had for his ladylove. The touching of lips, an age-old ritual between two people melded their souls. The words were like a re-enactment of the play Eric and I had shared together. My voice strained harder to sound normal. With the last word I closed the book.

Eric rose from the chair and came to me. "I owe you an apology, Meredith."

I was "Meredith" again.

"I expected to hear a silly tale of a maiden's woes," he said. "Instead, I heard a moving tale of intrigue and ... passion."

He offered me his hand and helped me to my feet. His glowing tribute stunned me. It was no longer necessary, but he still held my hand. The tingle singing down my limbs was just from sitting too long, I told myself.

"Are all of your stories so ... titillating?"

"They're all somewhat alike in that respect," I confessed.

His brow arched in a pleased response. "To think I've been reading the wrong books all these years ... "

I smiled. "Consider yourself educated."

"That, I do." Those distinctly chiseled features and hypnotic eyes seemed almost illegal for one man to possess. "One more question."

I shook my head. "I'm sorry. I believe the rules of the game state one question only. You've had yours now it's time for mine."

His eyelids narrowed suspiciously. "Go on."

My mouth felt dry. I swallowed. "If I could grant you one wish, what would it be?"

Eric's voice lowered to a husky whisper. "You like to jump right into the fire, don't you?" He released my hand and walked back to the desk and opened the bottom drawer. Pulling out a bottle and a glass from the drawer he offered me some whiskey.

I declined. "Chance nothing, gain nothing," I answered.

The bottle clanked against the glass. He poured himself two fingers worth and drank it in one swill. "And what do you hope to gain, Meredith?"

That was a good question. What did I hope to gain. Love? Respect? A chance at a fairy tale? "Perhaps just a glimpse of the real you."

"The real me?" He set the glass on the desk and poured himself another draught. "I think I'll take my chances with the consequences.

The liquor smelled bitter and sweet at the same time. "Very well, I want to stay here at Boothe House for the two months I originally planned."

Eric lifted the glass to his lips and stared at me from over the rim. A full minute passed before he answered. "Granted."

Graham sat up with a sleepy moan. "Why didn't someone wake me?"

"We didn't think you would hear us over all that snoring." Eric slammed the drawer and strode to the door. "I'm leaving in the morning, Graham. I'll back be in a few days."

Leaving? Eric was leaving? Instead of elation, I felt disturbingly depressed.

He then turned to me softening his harshness. "Good night, Meredith"

"Good night," I said softly. Had I said something wrong?

"Did I really snore?" Graham asked, sitting up and rubbing

his eyes.

"No," I assured him. "At least not loudly."

"Did I at least make it to the end of your story?"

I shook my head sympathetically. "Not quite." I tossed the book onto a chair and turned toward the fire. A chill ran over my bare arms. I didn't feel like playing games anymore.

He groaned. "What a dastardly thing to do. Would you start again? I promise to give you my undivided attention."

"Another time perhaps. I'm tired. I think I'll go on to bed." As I started walking toward the door, Graham reached out for my hand.

"You must hate me for being so rude," he said, his brown eyes pleading for forgiveness. "I wouldn't blame you if you never spoke to me again."

"I could never hate you."

"Promise?" he asked in earnest as if his fate were hinged on my answer.

"Promise."

I opened the door to my room that night with a heavy heart. Did Eric detest my presence so much that he'd rather leave his home than bear the sight of me? Was my pride too strong to let me stay?

Just as I had nearly convinced myself I had nothing to gain by remaining, the scent of ginger filled the room. Madelaine. I sprang to the dressing table and stared at the mirror. The rising ebb of anticipation made my pulse quicken. Disappointment made it sink. My own reflection stared back at me—nothing more. For an eternity of time I waited and wondered: would she come back? Or was it just my imagination?

As the mantel clock struck midnight, my eyelids began to droop. I stood and stretched, pulled a blanket off the bed, wrapped myself in it and sat in the tufted chair. From the chair I could see the mirror and Madelaine when she appeared. If I could just wait a little longer, she would come. I was sure of it. But I was tired; tired of playing games, tired of creating plots and tired of believing in fantasies. Would it really matter if I could prove I'd seen a ghost?

My eyelids fluttered. In that brief interlude, between darkness and light, I saw a feminine hand open a velvet covered book, heard the scratch of an ink pen as it scribed across the paper and read the words of a new beginning ...

๑ SIX ๑

May 24

Mrs. Edmund Ignacious Boothe. I write the words over and over again and yet, I can't believe it is true. I'm married. Was it only just yesterday? Edmund was so wonderful planning all the preparations. The wedding was smaller than Momma wanted but she understood Edmund's need for haste. He's been away from his practice now for nearly a month. A month doesn't seem very long, but it was long enough for two people to fall in love.

The train ride was long and uncomfortable, but we're home now

Home.

This is my home now. I'm mistress of Boothe House. It all sounds so strange. The house is so much grander than I expected, and dark. I'm not sure where I am to start. Edmund has been so understanding. He is a man of few words, but his gentleness and caring tell me of his devotion. I feel so blessed. He would like to have a child as soon as possible. A son. I think I shall start there. Nothing would make me happier.

The hand set the pen down and closed the book. With infinite care she placed the journal deep within the chest and replaced the false bottom. As she passed the mirror, I saw the bloom of radiance on the face of a new bride, the beautiful visage of a youthful Madelaine.

My eyes flew open and scanned the room. The mirror held a blank reflection and the air was void of perfume. It was just a dream, I told myself and nothing more. *But, mercy!* It seemed so real.

The mantel clock chimed again as I had heard it just before I closed my eyes. Time had moved swiftly. Dawn was approaching. Streaks of rose-hued light edged their way over the horizon bringing with them a promise of dry weather and sunlit skies.

With a groan I rose from the chair. It was an uncomfortable position in which to pass the night. My neck and head were stiff and sore, and my dress, rumpled and creased. I had transformed back into my pumpkin. It was bound to happen sooner or later. I preferred the later.

After a long soak in warm soothing water I felt considerably better. My head and neck still throbbed, but my gait was more relaxed. When I emerged from the bathroom I noticed that someone had been in my room. My book and an envelope had been placed on the bed while I bathed.

I opened the envelope and found a draft written for the rent I paid. It was for the full amount. "He didn't want to leave anything to chance. The cur." Swallowing my apprehension, I read the accompanying letter.

Dear Meredith,

I had hoped to see you before I left to give you this, but time would not allow it. I inquired of Graham the amount you paid. I trust it is correct. I could not, in good conscience, keep the money you forwarded for rent because in serving my consequences to stay last night, you also granted my wish. Please consider yourself a guest at Boothe House for as long as you wish.

The choice is now yours.

As you've probably guessed, I have alternative motives for keeping you here. I'm going through with your idea of a ball. Since I'm ill equipped at planning such an event, I look forward to hearing more of your ideas. I will be returning in a few days. I hope to see you then. If you choose to abandon your stay, I will understand and wish you well in your endeavors.

Eric

P.S. I took the liberty of reading the rest of your book. The stories were very good overall. Your instincts are remarkable. The characters seemed trite at times, however, and lacked the luster of your narration. I guess hearing the words by a poetic voice makes the difference. With a little improvement they may be a success.

What did he mean by *may* be a success? They were a success!

Opinion aside, being direct was a trait my father admired and shared. I could handle his criticism if he truly meant it; and if he truly meant he wanted me to stay, I could handle that, too. Gladly.

The prospect of continuing my work in my garden room made me anxious to start. I quickly dressed and set to work. The pen literally flew across the paper as I recalled the feelings of a bride settling in her new home. The dream became an instant inspiration.

When the sun moved to cast its ray upon the page, I realized that I had misjudged the hour. Breakfast had passed hours ago and now I found myself famished. It was time for a break anyway, I decided. The stiffness in my neck and shoulders had returned from hunching over the desk so long. Linnea would undoubtedly refuse to serve me at this inappropriate hour, but I was determined to get something to eat even if I had to fix it myself.

With the new bravado of being a welcomed guest, I went down to the kitchen. Linnea was noticeably absent, so I helped myself to a pot of tea and scones with cream.

My leisurely breakfast was soon disrupted by Graham's voice. Linnea and Ana entered at his heels. The cook stopped short when she saw the tea and scones before me. I held my ground and raised a brow in challenge. She pursed her thin lips into a blue line and moved on. A round finally won in my favor.

Graham centered his attention on the little housekeeper. "You can start at the top, I suppose, and work your way down," he suggested.

"All the rooms, sir?" Her eyes lit up in horror.

"Yes, Ana, every room in this house has to be made presentable."

The poor woman sneezed in response. She wiped at her snout with a rolled up handkerchief. "As you wish, sir."

"That's a good girl, Ana. I'm counting on you," Graham replied. "Meredith! What happened to you? I was beginning to worry."

"I was just in my room working."

"And how is your writing coming along?"

"Very well, thank you."

"Any chance of a preview?"

I shook my head. "None. Not until it's finished."

"And after all I've done for you!" he teased.

"And what might that be?" I inquired.

That devilish grin returned. "Come, and I'll show you."

He took my hand and led me to the front door. "Ready?"

"Yes!" Of course I was ready—ready to pop with curiosity.

When he opened the door, I squealed with delight. "Lucille!" She stood all spit and polished, ready for the road, not one spot marring her perfect complexion. "How did you get her up here?"

"It took a little doing, but with the help of our two nags I was able to pull her out of that rut. That's quite a machine you have there. Rolls Royce is it?"

"Yes, it was a gift from the Colonel."

"The Colonel?"

"My father," I explained. "He served in the royal forces for twenty years. The name just stuck with him. Anyway, he said he wanted to give me something special for my twenty-first birthday. He suggested I name her Lucille after my grandmother, the most sturdy and dependable woman he knew. She's lived up to it ever since."

"It fits her."

"Would you like to go for a ride?" I asked, anxious to get behind the wheel myself.

"I thought you'd never ask."

We took a short trip into the hills overlooking Hemlock. The air had warmed considerably. The sun felt like heaven against my face. The fiery colors of autumn amazed me. Looking down at the valley at the crimson and gold landscape, I was filled with anticipation for the change in seasons. "The snow must be lovely in the winter time. Do you think there'll be some in time for the ball?"

"Four weeks is a little soon for snow but ..."

"Four weeks?!" I assumed the ball would be in two months or so.

"That's precisely what I said."

"How can you possibly be ready in four weeks?"

Graham shrugged his shoulders. "I don't know. But Eric says we will be ready in four weeks, so ready we will be."

"You're not pleased."

"Pleased?" he snorted. "Not hardly. All he can think about is this blasted party!"

"I thought you liked the idea of a party."

"I did, but Eric insists on inviting all those would-be buyers. I don't like the idea of strangers moving into Boothe house.

Uncle Edmund will be terribly angry when he learns of this."

I blinked and cocked my head wondering if I had heard correctly. "Your Uncle? But I thought he was ... dead."

"He is."

"Then how can he ...?"

"Uncle Edmund knows everything that goes on in that house."

This was too much to believe. "Are you saying ...?"

"Of course, who do you think my chess partner is?"

There was a brief pause. Words escaped me. Then I saw the corner of Graham's mouth lift in amusement. "You're playing with me, aren't you?" I asked.

He chuckled. "I'm sorry. You just looked so serious."

"Well, you did have me going there for a moment."

"I wasn't jesting about selling the house. My uncle entrusted the place into my care. I hate to let him down."

"There was no way you could foresee your circumstances."

"I know. I haven't given up yet, though. There's still a chance I can keep it going. If not, well ... I hope Uncle Edmund will understand. He can be quite formidable when crossed."

"Graham—!" I shot in warning.

He smiled sheepishly. It was hard to tell when he was serious or not. "Linnea must be ready to serve lunch. We better hurry. I don't want to keep her waiting."

Graham was always late. Why was today an exception, I wondered.

As we approached the house I took inspection of the outside. It still seemed to frown even in the daylight from its arched entrance and tangled vines wrinkling its face. It was no wonder the inhabitants were so disagreeable. I found myself a bit depressed just passing through the portal.

We discussed the ball over lunch. Graham decided on a musketeer costume. There were plenty of costumes available to me also in the attic—if I chose to stay that long. A pack of hounds couldn't keep me away. I'd never been to a masquerade before. The idea excited me. But what would I wear? I wanted it to be special, something unique.

Graham devoured his second helping while I pushed aside my cold rations. I wasn't very hungry anyway. Excusing myself, I left Graham to his feasting and went upstairs. As I turned to go to my room I heard a strained groan. The noise originated from the opposite end of the hall. Ana, the housekeeper, was battling an uncooperative door, and the door was winning. Sprigs of grey dangling from her cap, her complexion ripened to a ruddy hue, she looked bedraggled and exhausted. There was no earthly way she was going to clean the entire house within four weeks. Taking pity on the woman I offered my assistance.

"Here, let me help you," I offered. "I can do this room. Why don't you take one of the others."

"It wouldn't be right for a guest to be doing the cleaning, Miss."

I held up my hand brooking no argument. "Lord Boothe asked for my help and I'm more than happy to lend it."

"But I'm sure he didn't mean for you to ..."

"Please, Ana, there's little time for argument."

"All right," she said. "If that's what you want. I'll not be arguing the matter. You're welcome to it. That room's been closed up for over five years; no telling what vermin lurks behind that door."

"May I?" I asked of her rags and waxing polish.

She gratefully handed them over. I turned the latch and pressed on the door. It was indeed stuck. Using my shoulder now I pushed again. It wouldn't budge. If I hadn't known better I would have sworn someone was pushing against it from the other side.

I tried again using my full weight. The door popped opened. An unusual rodent-like stench rushed out making me gasp. The room was dark as a crypt. I immediately went to the windows and thrust back the curtains. With determination and a few mumbled curses I loosened the stubborn latches and cast open the windows letting the fresh autumn breeze flow in. My lungs took in the welcomed air before I set myself to the task I misguidedly volunteered for.

It was the master bedroom, a very grand and masculine room. I sensed I had been in there before, but I was sure I hadn't. Each piece of furniture and decoration was familiar to me. I knew if I closed my eyes I could navigate through the room naming each piece.

In fact, I had crossed the room in total darkness when I entered, going directly to the windows without incident, yet there was a large, high backed chair and table in the path. How did I know they were there? How did I instinctively know to go around them? The implication set my mind to wonder.

The one object to verify my suspicions sat next to the armoire on the other side of the room, just where I knew it would be. Carefully removing the vase from on top, I pulled off the lace shawl that covered it. There was the wooden chest Madelaine lovingly tended. Kneeling down in front of it I took a deep breath and lifted the heavy lid. It squeaked to a stop, fully open. There were piles of yellowing blankets and linens. I quickly removed them and felt the bottom with my hand as I remembered Madelaine doing in my dream. My heart pounded with anxious trepidation when I found the notch in the wood. I pried my fingernail into the notch and lifted the false bottom. Hidden in its secret place, where it had sat for so many years was the crimson, velvet-covered journal. With shaky hands I lifted the precious book to my lap. I stared at the gold signature M on the cover for a long moment, too frightened of what I might find inside. Gearing up my courage, I opened the cover and read the words written in Madelaine's own hand. I held my breath as I turned the pages knowing I had read them before. It was there, word for word, the passage she had written in my dream.

The answer was all too clear. Madelaine had indeed passed on. She revealed herself to me in spirit because she could not do so in the flesh. Into my dreams she had crept, revealing her life, her most intimate thoughts.

I didn't want to believe it. I tried hard not to, but the evidence before me was too hard to ignore. I fought hard to quell the fear that rose hackles on my skin. Why me? A complete stranger? There were several people in the house ... unless ... something frightened her. "Something or someone."

Clouds drifted into the path of the sun. The room grew dark. I could hear the howling of the wind grow louder with each second. The curtains billowed and arched. Wind moved through the room like a gale and slammed the door shut with finality.

Silence.

As if all sound had been locked in a sealed vault, the room hung completely still.

It started as a small scratching against bricks, a light scrape, a creak, a cry. The noise intensified to a cackle, inhuman in sound and evil with intent. My eyes darted to the portrait of Edmund Ignacious Boothe over the mantel. His painted eyes seemed to stretch and bulge, staring at me with accusation. This was no dream.

I raced to the door. The latch turned but the door would not open. "Ana?"

I pulled and pulled at the door. "Ana! Open the door!"

The cackling grew louder, echoing through the room, the sound so loud it drowned out the erratic thudding in my chest. My hands covered my ears to block out the horrible pitch.

Pressure wrapped around my neck, pulling tight, making me gasp. My lungs tried to inhale but the effort made me dizzy and weak. I couldn't breathe. My fingers clawed at the cords contracting my throat. I felt nothing but my own flesh, yet the pressure increased.

Was this how Madelaine died?

With the last vestiges of oxygen in my lungs, I screamed "Ana!" then slumped into a black abyss.

✦ SEVEN ✦

I don't remember how I came to be in my garden room. I only remember opening my eyes to Graham's gentle coaxing and seeing his worried frown.

"What happened?" My voice sounded oddly groggy.

"You fainted," Graham answered. "How do you feel?"

"Confused."

His boyish face leaned closer. He smiled. "That's understandable. Ana came for me and said you had locked yourself in the master bedroom. You gave me quite a fright when I saw you lying there on the floor."

"I fainted?" It was all coming back to me, the wind, the horrible cackling and—the journal. My eyes quickly searched the room. "Where is it?"

"Where's what?" Graham asked.

"The ..." No. It was better to keep silent about the journal. How would Graham react to my snooping around? It was very possible that he did not even know of the journal's existence. "Nothing ... I left some rags and things in the room."

"I'll have Ana take care of that. I think you've done enough cleaning for the day. I had Linnea bring up some soup. It's even hot."

His levity did little to ease my discomfort. "I'm not very hungry." I tried to sit up but my head began to throb. I fell back down. A shooting pain ran down my spine to the pit of my stomach. My hand went to the back of my head and found a

66

walnut sized lump. "Ouch!"

"Here, let me see," Graham offered. He leaned over and parted my hair with care. "You have quite a knot there. You must have hit your head on the floor. It doesn't look too serious."

"But it's huge!"

"Better to have it pop out than in. Does it hurt?"

Did a dental drill to an abscessed tooth hurt? I nodded, keeping my surly comments to myself. It was not his fault; being abed with illness brought out the worst in me. I had never been a complacent patient.

He reached for a glass on the table. "Drink this."

I looked at the chalky white liquid. "What is it?"

"Something to help you rest."

I stared at it, uncertain.

"I'm a doctor, remember?"

"No, you're not."

"Well, almost. Drink up. I promise it will make you feel better."

Anxious for any relief, I downed the liquid. "I'm sorry to be such a bother. I've probably taken up enough of your time."

"Don't be foolish. Your health means more than a few loose floorboards. I can fix them later."

"Please, you don't have to stay. I'm feeling better."

"Are you sure?"

I nodded, forgetting myself, and winced from the pain.

He frowned. "You promise not to get up from this bed?"

"I promise." I didn't think I could even if I wanted to. I was feeling sleepy all of a sudden.

"I'll come back in a little while. Now remember, you promised."

With a yawn, I inclined my head and waved.

He leaned over and ever so gently pressed his lips to my forehead. It was a warm gesture. I smiled, my eyelids growing heavy. The concoction was beginning to work. The pain ebbed.

"Pleasant dreams," was the last thing I remembered as his

lips brushed briefly against mine.

My haunted dreams returned in a tangled pattern. They confused me, leaping from one emotion to another like a revolving kaleidoscope. Madelaine was joyous and happy one moment then strangely frightened, running away from some evil force threatening to overpower her. Her thoughts became my own. I felt her gaiety and sense of peril. But the jumbled pictures did not make any sense.

She finished a page in her journal and closed the book. Her eyes strayed to me, beseeching me to understand. A tear fell to her pale cheek. I felt so helpless. Her hand rested on the closed journal. It was then that I understood. The journal. I had to get the journal.

The visions faded. I tried to emerge from my drug-induced sleep but my head felt leaden. My eyelids fluttered as I tried to focus. It was a moment before I became fully awake. The room was different. I had been asleep many hours. It was nearly midnight. But there was something else, another presence in the room—Madelaine. There was no visible sign of her, but her scent was still strong and vibrant in the air. I breathed deeply of the sweet ginger, convincing myself that it was really true. There was a safe feeling about her being so near. It saddened me though that she was no longer of this life, and that we would meet only in spirit.

The door creaked open. It was Graham. I shut my eyes and pretended to be asleep. His footfalls approached the bed. He hesitated. Could he smell her too, I wondered. He then leaned over to place another kiss upon my lips. It was gentle and soft, not the least bit passionate, yet his affection was evident. My eyelids stayed tightly shut. I was uncertain how I felt about his ardent display. I had not considered him in that fashion. Or had I? My mind was so confused. I was losing track of my objective.

He didn't stay long. After readjusting the blanket about my shoulders he blew out the lamp and quietly closed the door behind him. I waited a good amount of time to make sure he had disappeared before I rose from the bed. The room swayed as I stood. I reached over to the table and knocked over the glass that had held the potent drink Graham had given me. I caught it just before it hit the floor. The drink was much too strong for my liking but it had worked. My head still hurt, but with a dull ache now instead of piercing shards of pain.

The hall was clear. With lamp in hand, I padded down in stocking feet to the master bedroom. My hand rested on the latch, but I could not seem to move. Recalling the events that happened when I was last in there, I froze. The floor seemed to sway under my feet. Perhaps I acted too hastily in going there at that time of night. No! I scolded myself. I would not turn and run.

I turned the latch and pushed hard on the door. It opened—almost too easily. I stood in the safety of the doorway and raised the lamp to search the room. It was eerily quiet. Shadows moved about as I moved the lamp. Not wanting to let my imagination wander, I quickly went to the chest. It was closed. The vase and shawl were neatly back in place. The wood was even smoothly polished. In fact, the whole room smelled freshly clean.

I opened the chest and frantically searched for the journal. It was gone. I looked around, opening drawers and looking under papers. It was not there. My eyes were drawn to the portrait of Edmund. I could not see his face in the dark but I knew he still stared at me with hatred. "What did you do with it?" I accused.

Now I was truly losing my mind. Did I expect an answer?

Receiving one would have no doubt sent me screaming into the hall. There was no use in looking any longer. The journal was not there. I would have to wait until morning to ask Ana. She must have placed it somewhere when she cleaned the room.

Madelaine was gone from my garden room. The scent of spice had vanished. There was nothing else to do but go back to bed. Both my mind and body were exhausted. I changed into my nightgown and crawled under the sheets. I closed my eyes hoping to see Madelaine. She didn't come.

Morning eventually dawned, and I with it. I waited in my room, scrawling a few thoughts on paper until I heard a familiar sneeze down the hall.

Ana's eyes narrowed as she saw me approach. "I hope you're not wanting to help again."

"No," I sighed. I realized my fainting was more of a hindrance than help but I hadn't planned it that way. "I just have a question for you."

"If it won't take too long ..."

"... I want to know if you saw the red journal in the master bedroom."

She thought for a moment then shook her head. "No, there's no red journal."

"It belongs in the chest. I may have left it out."

"In the chest you say?" she asked. I nodded hopefully. She raised her snout in the air. "I don't pry into personal belongings."

As if I do? And I did, but that was beside the point. "Didn't you see it when you cleaned the room?"

"I didn't clean the room."

"Then who did?"

"Master Graham. He said he would clean up after your—mishap."

Graham? Then he found the journal. "Damn!"

She frowned.

"I'm sorry," I apologized. "I still don't feel all that well. Thank you for your time." The pain in my head increased. There was no reason to panic. I would simply go to Graham and politely ask him for the journal. He in turn would wonder why I wanted it. For research maybe? Having only hatred for the woman, he may not have even read it. Not bloody likely! He was no doubt dying of curiosity as I was.

What was I to do? If Madelaine had wanted Graham to read it she would have revealed herself to him and not me.

Time to panic.

I went to the most likely place I could think of—his room.

I felt uncomfortable looking through his things. It was most unbecoming of a guest. As luck would have it, I found the journal in a drawer by his bedside, a natural place to put bedtime reading material.

I was about to steal it away to the privacy of my room when I stopped. I was acting like a common thief. What would Graham do when he found the journal missing? The inquiry would ultimately lead to me. The consequences were too mortifying to consider. After all Graham's kindness to me, I couldn't betray him like that. I was sure he had read some—if not most—of the journal already, so there was no reason now to shield it from his eyes. It was best to ask Graham for it outright. I owed him that much.

The journal sat so temptingly in my hands. The pages fell open. My eyes were instantly drawn to the familiar scribe.

The first month of their marriage seemed truly happy. Madelaine's writing glowed with contentment. She overcame her apprehensions and embraced her new life. Hemlock embraced her in return.

The villagers often gave her token gifts they crafted by hand in appreciation for a kindness that she bestowed upon them. She treasured their friendship and it was to them she turned when loneliness caught up with her.

June 11

Edmund went to town today and may not be back for several days. It is his third trip since we've returned. It's selfish of me to want to keep him here by my side. I hoped we would spend more time together. I will miss him, but it gives me a chance to visit the village again. Poor Mr. Dobbs hobbled with his gout again. I shall have to remember to bring him some buckram oil to put into his brandy tomorrow. Momma said it is a cure-all for what ails you.

I brought a basket of blush roses I clipped this morning from the greenhouse for Aggie. She mentioned how much she loved them. I wanted to cheer her up after the passing of her father-in-law. I wanted to go to the services, but Edmund wouldn't hear of it. It seems the elder Mr. Towns and Edmund did not get on well. I hope Aggie and Duff understand.

I met a new friend today. Her name is Sarah Bradley. She too is recently married and new to Hemlock. Her husband, Ian, is a very dear man. Sarah and I spent hours getting to know one another, and he never once complained, even though his dinner was kept waiting. Edmund would have disapproved, but Ian seemed genuinely pleased that Sarah and I got on so well.

Oh, it was such a lovely afternoon! I feel a special kinship with Sarah. Talking and sharing secrets with someone again makes me less homesick, especially now when I miss my home more than ever.

Reluctantly, I closed the book and placed it back in the drawer. It would be tempting fate if I chanced reading more. Once I asked Graham for it personally I could read it at length in my own room. Finding Graham to ask him was another matter.

After my futile search of the house I broke down and went to the most reliable source. Linnea seemed to worship every movement Graham made. I supposed she knew when and where the man lived and breathed every second of the day. She wasn't likely to give me his whereabouts willingly, though. I found her in the kitchen fixing a basket lunch. She looked at me suspiciously as I approached with the smile I save for incorrigible children. "Linnea that's kind of you, but you don't have to go to all that trouble. I'll just have my lunch in the dining room."

Her mouth curved up in a wan smile. "This basket is for

Master Graham. If you want lunch you'll have to wait until after I deliver this to him."

"I'll be happy to take it to him in my motorcar," I offered.

"To the barn?" she eyed me queerly.

"You're right, how silly of me. I'll just walk." I whisked the basket from her hands and rushed out the door brushing off her protests.

I walked around to the back of the house in what I hoped was the general direction of the barn. The staccato sound of a distant hammer echoed through the open air. I followed it toward the lake. The tall grasses opened up to a spacious paddock where two horses gaily romped kicking their heels up in the summer-like air.

"Graham?" I called. The hammering stopped. I waited what seemed like an eternally long time. I began to wonder if I had the right barn and was about to head back when Graham's head appeared over the rooftop. I lifted the basket. "I brought your lunch!"

His grin broadened. One way to gain Graham's attention was through his stomach. "I'll be right down."

He came, wiping the sweat from his brow; his shirt opened to the waist. I remembered the kiss he lightly bestowed on my lips and was drawn to looking at him in a new light. There was a playful attractiveness about him. Visions of another man entered my mind—Eric. How their kisses differed.

"How's your head?" he asked me.

"Fine," I lied.

He took the basket from my arm. "This is heavy. You shouldn't have carried this all the way down here. Linnea could have done it."

"I wanted to."

"You will join me, won't you?"

"I thought you'd never ask!" He led me to a vacant stool in the barn. I accepted the sandwich he offered but only nibbled at it. The queasiness in my stomach had yet to dissipate. "Are the horses out there the only two you have?"

"This old barn had ten at one time. They were sold off one by one. Those two are the last ones. They still have a few good years left in them. I'll have to take you riding. You do ride, don't you?"

"Of course." The idea of a bone-jarring ride did not appeal to me at that moment. "But not today if you don't mind. I don't think my head could take it."

His face grew concerned. "Does it pain you?" He wasted no time in parting my hair to examine my injury.

"Maybe just a little." I yelped in pain when he touched the tender spot. "All right, maybe a lot."

"Sorry. It looks better, but I still think you should take it easy. Lean forward."

"Ouch! I have been. The drink you gave me last night seemed to work. Ouch! Now what are you doing?"

"Just checking for swelling and thankfully it's gone down." He replaced my hair, his fingertips resting on my neck. "You're my best patient."

"I'm your only patient." I turned to him. Without warning, his lips covered mine in a gentle kiss. Maybe I should have turned away but I didn't. Curiosity led me to compare. Graham paled against his cousin. When we parted I did look away.

"I'm sorry. I shouldn't have done that," he apologized.

"No, that's all right," I rushed to assure him.

"Then you're not angry that I kissed you?"

"No, of course not, it's just that I don't think we ..."

"It's Eric then, isn't it?"

"Eric?" Merciful heavens! What made him think of that?

"You're in love with him aren't you? I can't say I'm surprised. You wouldn't be the first—or the last."

In love? With Eric? The idea was simply ludicrous. "But that's—"

He went on unmindful of my protests. "Most women can't help but be."

"I'm not like most women," I tried to assure him.

"I know. That's what I was counting on. Eric, too, apparently."

"Graham—"

"I'm sorry. I don't mean to sound bitter. It's just that I don't want you to get hurt. And you will, you know. He may encourage you at first, but he'll only break your heart in the end. It's his way. Some type of revenge against his mother, I think."

"Really, Graham, your concern for my welfare is very noble, but it's not necessary. I hardly know Eric. Or even you for that matter."

"That can be remedied." He took my hand and brought it to his grinning lips.

"That's not what I meant."

"Please Meredith, all I ask is to be given a chance. I know I don't have much to offer ..."

"It's not that," I protested.

"Good! Then I won't take no for an answer." He kissed the palm of my hand. "I promise you won't be sorry."

I was utterly flattered, and his charm was not completely lost on me. I would be a fool to refuse. Wouldn't I? "All right."

He was in such a jovial mood I thought it was as good a time as any to bring up the journal. "Graham, when I was cleaning your uncle's bedroom I came across a journal. I only read the first few pages, but it piqued my curiosity. I was wondering if I could possibly read the rest. I think it might help to inspire me."

"What journal is this?" he asked.

"The red velvet one with the initial 'M' on it. Ana said you cleaned the room after me, so I assumed you knew where it was. I left it by the chest. Surely you must have seen it."

"I think that bump to your head affected your memory. I didn't see anything like what you described."

"But ...?" How could I accuse him of lying without incriminating myself?

He turned to me with a look that held no humor. "There was no journal Meredith."

๑๑ EIGHT ๑๑

Why would he lie? What was in that journal he did not want me to read? I pondered that question while pacing in my room. If he were so against my reading it he could have offered some excuse. Instead, he wanted me to believe the journal never existed, that I had imagined seeing it. It was a slight I could not easily ignore.

Good sense told me to put the matter to rest, to put the entire house and all its ghostly presence behind me. Part of me wanted to pack up my pens and paper and be gone, but the other part, the part that never listened to reason, refused to give up. This part also propelled me down the hall back into Graham's room. I knew he would not be there. I had left him at the barn with several hours' work ahead of him.

I was back to where I was before, sneaking into another's private domain. Playing such a devious role was not to my liking, but Graham had left me no choice. The crystal brandy decanter on top of the bed table hobbled as I opened the drawer. Steadying it, I looked over my shoulder, worrying someone surely had heard the deafening noise. The sight of the journal whetted my curiosity so much I quickly overcame my fear. With a deep breath and a conviction I was doing what Madelaine wanted me to do, I opened the book. The entries became fewer and more brief.

In the writing before me I saw no evidence of a scheming vindictive woman; Madelaine was but a kind and gentle soul, loved by all who knew her—all but one.

June 21
Edmund came home today. I put on my new dress and made sure all of his favorite dishes were prepared. He was too preoccupied in his work to notice. I couldn't seem to entice him away from his evening brandy, either. His "elixir of life" seems to hold more appeal to him than I do. He didn't even kiss me good night.

June 27
He's changed.

July 2
I went for a walk today, alone again. Edmund seems to have lost interest in our walks together. I miss that. I went to see Sarah. She's expecting a baby come winter. I'm very happy for her and a bit envious too.

July 19
It was Edmund's birthday today. I had the library refurbished during his last trip as a surprise. He was quite upset that I had changed the decor his father and grandfather loved for so many years. His anger frightened me. But it was my own fault. Whether the room needed it or not, I should have asked his permission.
September 3
Sarah has finally begun to show. Ian is stumbling over himself to ease her burden.
I am still without child.

October 16

We have begun preparations for the ball. There are so many things to do. I'm happy for the diversion. It shall be exciting, I think. I've never attended a masquerade. This will be my first affair as mistress of Boothe House. I hope I do not let Edmund down.

October 31

All Hallow Eve. The village is having the traditional Halloween festival tonight. It sounds like such fun, eating, dancing and a bonfire, too. Aggie even lent me a peasant costume to wear. Edmund strictly forbids me to go. I do so hate to miss it!

November 1

I went to the festival while Edmund slept. It was wrong of me, I know, and I didn't stay long, but I had a marvelous time! It was such fun to laugh again.

November 3

It was a frantic day making sure everything was in readiness. Edmund was away most of the day. I had hoped he would remain home and offer his assistance, since this is our first party, but he made it clear as he did from the beginning that the preparations were the responsibility of the lady of the manor. Given the impressive guest list, I pray in keeping with the Boothe tradition it will be a success. It must be. Edmund will have it no other way.

November 4

The ball was wonderful! And so was Edmund. I had worried these past months if maybe I had been a disappointment to him. But last night my worries were all for naught. He led me proudly on his arm to welcome all the guests. And when we danced, he held me close, looking down at me with the smile I had almost forgotten. Perhaps I worry too much.

"Eh, hmm!"

The sound startled me. I looked up to see Ana in the doorway with a frown on her face. Heat of embarrassment rose to my cheeks. "I found the journal."

"So I see."

"I was just looking for Mr. Ferguson when I—"

"There's no need to explain. It's not my business." She went on to place the clean handkerchiefs from her arm into the bureau drawer.

She stood there folding and unfolding, taking her time. I understood the hint. I replaced the journal and smoothed my skirt. "I'll see if he's downstairs."

"Mm, hmm," she nodded and smiled.

I prayed the little housekeeper would keep to herself about catching me in Graham's room. I was almost certain she would. Minding her own business was a trait on which she prided herself.

The atmosphere in the house was closing in on me. I needed some air and distance from its probing eyes. Lucille was waiting for me. We took a short trip into the village and pulled up outside Croakers.

I spotted Aggie behind the bar and waved a greeting. She joined me at a table by the window with a welcoming pot of tea. "I'm glad to see you safe and sound," she said.

"Why? Did you think I wouldn't be?" I asked

"I worried about you leaving here alone, especially when you don't know your way around. These roads can be treacherous, you know. I'm happy to see you've fared well."

"Indeed I have."

"Then you like it there at Boothe House?"

"It wasn't exactly how I pictured it but, yes, I do like it," I answered honestly.

"And they're treating you kindly?"

"Yes, why?" I wondered about her odd questioning.

"I don't mean to frighten you, dearie. Those folks just haven't been known for their hospitality. We don't see much of them. They keep to themselves."

"They've been very nice to me. Most of them anyway. Linnea, their cook, seems to have taken a disliking to me, though I don't know why."

"Oh, she's a nasty one. Always was. She puts on airs because she works in the big house. They only kept her because young Graham took a liking to her."

"She does dote on him," I remarked.

"What about the other one, the dark one? He's back isn't he?"

"Yes," I nodded. "Eric was there but he left for a few days on business."

"He's a handsome one."

I couldn't have agreed more. But Graham was nice looking too. I couldn't discount that.

"Got his mother's dark looks he does. I think that was a sour pill for the elder Boothe. Never could understand why he always sent the boy away to school. Even when he was just a babe. Nearly broke his mother's heart it did."

"Tell me about her."

Aggie leaned back in her chair. She was in her element now: teller of village news. Her eyes softened fondly. "Oh, Madelaine was a lovely girl. Always had a smile. They were a striking pair, Lord Boothe with his Viking looks and Madelaine with her bonnie blue eyes."

"There was quite a stir that spring. Lord Boothe leaves on a

holiday and returns a few weeks later with a wife on his arm.
I mean it was all so sudden. There was talk at first; after a few
months and no sign of a babe, well, the rumor died down.
Madelaine would have liked nothing more. She was quite
disappointed she didn't conceive right off. When Master Eric
finally arrived she was so happy. Lord Edmund was pleased to
have a son, but as the boy grew to resemble the mother, he sent
him away for schooling. He wanted a Boothe you see, a fair-
haired heir to carry on the name. I think that's about the time
young Graham came to live with them."

"Where are his parents?"

Aggie leaned closer to whisper. "The mother died in an
asylum. She lost her mind after Graham was born. If you ask
me, I don't think she was quite right from the beginning. There's
a vein of insanity running through that family."

"And the father?"

"I don't know about him. All I know is Lord Boothe received
a telegram about his sister and went to fetch the boy."

"Did Graham and Eric become close then?" I wanted to
know what may have caused the riff between them.

"I suppose so. Eric was away at school most of the time.
Graham had a tutor. They seemed like amiable boys. Eric was
the more serious of the two. Graham didn't have the pressure of
being the Boothe heir. I think he may have been a bit jealous of
that too. Eric was clearly Madelaine's favorite. She would bring
him to the village when he was home. He and Sarah Bradley's
boy Sean would run about with the sheep. She never brought
Graham, though."

"What happened to her?"

"No one knows for sure. She just up and left one day."

"For no reason?"

"Oh, I'm sure his lordship gave her good reason. Always
being away, never a kind word. Madelaine would make excuses
that his work was very demanding."

"Graham mentioned he was a barrister."

"And a good one from what I heard. But then, evil minds think alike."

"You don't like the Boothes very much, do you?"

"There's nothing to like about them. Cursed lot, they are."

"Hey Aggie! How's 'bout an ale for a tired and thirsty old man." A middle-aged man had entered the pub taking a seat by the hearth. I knew who he was the moment he stepped through the door. He had aged twenty years, but he still fit Madelaine's description of the smithy, Chester McVickers.

"I'll be right wit' ya!" she called over her shoulder. "I'll just be a minute," she turned back to me. "Can I freshen that up for you?" she asked pointing to the teapot.

"No, it's fine, thank you."

With her eyes wrinkled up in a friendly smile, she nodded. "I'll be right back."

I poured myself another cup and sipped at it letting the warmth soothe my throat. I had learned a little more about Madelaine, but the reason for her disappearance was still a mystery. I wasn't about to believe Graham's version of another man until I had proof.

Aggie returned with a plate of powdered teacakes. I gratefully took one, finding my appetite had returned.

"Now where was I?" she asked taking her seat and wiping her hands on her apron.

"You were explaining why you disliked the Boothes," I offered with a mouthful of the delicious cake.

"Oh yes. They're an odd family. The grandfather, Ignacious Boothe, used to worship bad weather. He'd walk about at night in the pouring rain. Got himself killed that way. The old man was hobbling along with his cane one night when he was run over." Her voice lowered. "They say you can still see his ghost hobbling about when it rains."

The hunchback on the road. "You don't believe in ghosts do you?"

"All I know is what people have told me they've seen. Some

even say Edmund's ghost roams the house looking for the wife who left him. And if he finds her it will be murder he's after."

"Sounds like silly superstition to me," I said, though after my experience in that house I was apt to believe it.

"Well, I haven't witnessed it myself, but rumors like this don't make themselves up, you know. Have you seen any strange goings on up there?"

I wasn't about to admit it and add fuel to the fire. "No."

"Madelaine herself thought there was something peculiar about that place. She said she felt someone or something was always looking over her shoulder."

I knew the feeling well. "Do you think she'll ever come back?" The question seemed relative when I already knew the answer.

"No," Aggie said sadly. "If she were able to she would have come back for her boy long ago."

"It's a sad story," I commented. "I would have liked to meet Madelaine."

"You would have liked her. You know … now that I look at you, you look a bit like her. It's in the smile. All you pretty young girls have that wonderful smile. If you want to know more about Madelaine you'll have to ask Sarah Bradley. They were close, those two. Sarah comes in here once a week for a chat. Now that Ian has passed away she doesn't know what to do with herself. I'm sure she'd love a visit."

I was saddened to hear of Ian's passing but excited to learn Sarah still lived in Hemlock. "Where does she live?"

"Her's is the first farm you see when coming to Hemlock from the south. The barn is white with a new roof the men folk just finished with."

"Do you think she will talk to me?"

"Just tell her Aggie sent you, then she'll probably talk your ear off like I'm doing now." She chuckled.

"I don't mind. I enjoyed it."

"So did I. It's not often we get a new face to look at. Everyone here already knows everyone else's business. There's nothing to talk about. You'll have to came back and fill me in on what's going on in the city."

"I'd like that," I replied.

"You'll have to come to our festival next week, too. We have it every Halloween. There'll be roast hog, dancing and a great bon fire. It's been a tradition since the 1600s. We don't burn hemlock anymore, though. It was plentiful back then. The valley was covered with it. There's no trace of it now. We burn the hay instead. It's just as well. If the eatin' of hemlock didn't kill you, the smell of it would. It gives off a hideous odor. You'd think you were being overrun by rats." She wrinkled her nose. "Here I go again, rambling on when I've got chores to do. You go ahead and visit Sarah. She'll be happy to have someone to talk to, and give her my best will you?"

"Of course," I replied. "Aggie, I just have one more question for you. Where can I have this posted. I've written a letter to let my father know I've arrived safely."

"Oh you've just missed today's delivery. I can hold onto it 'till tomorrow if you'd like."

"Would you?"

"Consider it done."

"Thank you. I'm sure he's waiting expectantly for word from me. I'll be sure to tell Sarah you said hello."

"And tell her thanks for the mint jelly from me."

"I will." The sun had gone behind the clouds making the air cooler. I closed my wrap about me and started Lucille's engine. She purred like clockwork. I gazed up at the clouds and the fleeting sun judging the time. Graham would surely be wondering about me.

I really should head back, I thought. I really should. The wheels turned onto the road toward the Bradley farm.

❧ NINE ❧

A woman slight of frame appeared in the window. She brushed aside a stray wisp of sliver hair that had once been colored gold by the sun. Her hazel eyes, tired yet clear, still held the country sparkle known to her. This was Sarah.

She seemed hesitant at first, but when I mentioned Aggie's name her face lit up in a broad smile. She kindly invited me in and went to fix a pot of tea.

It was a comfortable home—not large by any means—but suitable for a small family. There was no pretense or garishness about the decor, just simple life displayed in hand-woven blankets and well worn furniture.

A gallery of pictures hung on the parlor wall: one of Sarah and a handsome young man, a relative perhaps; another of two strapping boys, Ian and Sarah's sons, Jonathan and Sean; and a striking picture of a young Ian dressed in his finery with Sarah at his side in a gown of white—a wedding portrait complete with orange blossoms. They looked so happy, ready to start a new life together.

The pain of his passing was still evident in the creases of Sarah's eyes. It reminded me of when my mother died. It was the first time I had seen my father weep. He was different after that, like a small flame of hope had been suddenly extinguished. I could tell by the jut of her chin that Sarah tried her best to carry on.

Talking of Madelaine brought the smile back to her face.

"I remember when my eldest, Jonathan, was born, " Sarah said with wistful reminiscence. "Madelaine stayed by my side the whole time, holding my hand and listening to my prattle. Ian was so nervous he didn't know what to do with himself. Madelaine gave him all sorts of silly chores to keep him occupied. She even had him whittling down candles for extra string." Her laughter carried a longing for happier memories. "Do you have any children?"

"No, I'm not married," I confessed. "I haven't met the right man, yet."

"Oh, I'm sorry." She patted my hand in comfort. "You will and when you do you'll know it right here," she said pointing to her heart. "Yes, Ian and I were truly blessed. When Jonathan came along he was so happy to have a son. I think he secretly wanted a little girl, mind you," she winked, "but he was just as proud of our Jonathan. When Madelaine placed the babe in his arms for the first time I thought he was going to faint dead away. But he didn't. He cradled his son in his arms like it was the most natural thing.

"Madelaine had tears in her eyes as she watched them. I had been so wrapped up in my joy I hadn't considered Madelaine's feelings. She was happy for us, of course, but I could see the longing in her eyes for a child of her own. It was such a blessing then when little Eric was born. Madelaine was the happiest I had ever seen her."

"Was she very unhappy before that?" I asked.

The older woman paused, choosing her words carefully. "Madelaine was not one to complain. She didn't like to burden people with her own problems. But there were times when— oh, I don't know how to explain it, but sometimes not saying something can be the most telling of all." She glanced in the teapot. "Can I get you more tea?"

Hiding my grimace I shook my head. I had consumed enough tea during the entire day to drown a cow. "No, thank you. Please go on. What happened after Eric was born? Was Lord Boothe pleased?"

"Pleased?" she pondered the word. "Satisfied would be a better word for it. He took charge of the boy from day one. He hired a nurse. Madelaine was only allowed a few hours of the day with her child. His lordship didn't want the boy to grow up weak from a mother's influence. But Madelaine was a crafty woman. Every evening at six o'clock when the baby was put to bed—it didn't matter whether he was sleepy or not, he was kept to a very tight schedule—Madelaine would go to his room and shower her love on him. And it was she who got up in the middle of the night if he were hungry or restless. Edmund forbid the nurse to go to the babe during the night. He thought it would strengthen the boy's character to cry and go hungry. Can you imagine that?" she asked, clearly appalled.

No, I couldn't imagine anything so cruel.

"He thought he was right too, never hearing the baby complaining at night. He never considered the fact his wife would go against his wishes and care for the baby. Madelaine was usually obedient, but when it came to her son she blew all caution to the wind."

I sympathized with Madelaine's plight and applauded her bravery. "Did Edmund ever find out?"

"No. Madelaine disciplined herself to act in accordance with his strict standards, but only in his presence, mind you. She was a crafty one, indeed. When Edmund was assured she would not be a threat to the boy he dismissed the nurse and allowed her to care for Eric.

"Her victory didn't last long, though. When Eric turned five he was sent away for schooling."

"Was he never allowed home?" I asked.

"Oh, yes. Madelaine saw to it that he was home most weekends and holidays. That was her only time with him, and she spent every moment to the fullest. It would break her heart though to see him leave again. I asked her once if she ever tried to keep her son from going away and you know what she said?

'I would if I thought it best for him, but I'd rather suffer the separation than see him suffer in that house. It was the only time she hinted there was something wrong in Boothe House."

"Then she truly did love him as a mother should?" I asked.

"There's never been a doubt," Sarah defended. "As if it should be questioned at all."

"I'm sorry. I for one believe you. It's just that I heard—"

"Oh, I know what you've heard and it boils my blood. Madelaine would do anything for that boy."

"Even leave?"

The subject took a different turn making Sarah uncomfortable and reluctant to speak. "More tea?" she asked in a shaky voice.

I shook my head and placed my hand over hers to keep her from fleeing my question. "Sarah, why did she leave? Was it for another man?"

Her eyes widened. "Who told you that?"

"Her nephew Graham," I said. "He implied she was unfaithful."

Sarah's lips crimped in disgust. "Madelaine was a good woman! A good mother and a good wife, as much as that man would let her be."

"Then why did she leave?"

She looked down at the rumpled apron in her lap clutched tightly in her hand. She seemed to have aged a decade in the span of a few seconds. She shook her head but she would not meet my eyes. "I don't know."

"Surely you must have some idea?" I coaxed.

"I'm sorry. I can't help you."

Or won't. She was holding something back. She was not about to reveal a sacred trust to a total stranger. I would have to be satisfied with the story she gave me—for the moment anyway.

Lucille led me home as if she knew what was on my mind. I couldn't help but wonder what Madelaine's life was like being kept away from her son and being married to a man like

Edmund. He seemed to be a man obsessed with having a son, a perfectionist who mastered control of his life and of those around him.

And then there was Eric, the little boy whom I had comforted in my arms in a dream and the man who crept into my mind and refused to leave. He seemed to be the key to the whole mystery. Now if only I could unlock the door.

Dusk had come and gone and I was faced with returning to Boothe House in the dark. The edifice had resumed its sinister cloak not normally seen in the daylight. When I entered I felt like a trespasser once again in a place where I didn't belong, a place that didn't want me to belong.

I could feel Edmund's domineering presence. It had always been there, but now I could put a name to it. It was in every room like a deathly pall hovering overhead threatening to drop—in every room but one, my garden room. That was the haven I sought. The throbbing in my head had returned. I wanted nothing more than to seek the solace of my bed for some much needed rest.

"Meredith! There you are!" I whirled on the stairs to see Graham in the entrance to the library, cleaned and fresh, looking quite dapper. "I was beginning to worry. When you didn't come back for supper I thought something happened to you."

"Nothing happened. I just went into the village and lost track of time."

"You look pale. Come in here by the fire." He led me by the hand to the chair by the hearth. "I'll get you some tea."

"No! I mean, I don't really care for any, thank you. I'm a little tired. I thought I would just go up to my room and—"

"Oh. I was hoping to persuade you into a game of cards or checkers if you prefer, but if you'd rather not ..."

He looked so forlorn I didn't have the heart to refuse. "No, that's all right. A game of checkers sounds lovely."

"Good." He smiled. "But I have to warn you, I'm the champion in these parts."

"We'll see about that. Break out the board," I challenged.

The evening was enjoyable, but then, Graham was always an entertaining companion. I won every game. Graham's losses were a little obvious, but I guessed it was a ploy to gain my sympathy. I spared him none.

The yawn came regardless of my efforts to quell it. Graham took pity on me and escorted me to my room. He stood at my door looking at me expectantly. I knew what he was going to say before he even opened his mouth.

"Meredith, would you object to … I mean, would you mind if I … kissed you?"

Mind? Of course I didn't mind. I welcomed it, in fact. I needed something to wipe the memory of Eric's kiss clear of my head. "Yes."

"You would mind?" Graham asked, disappointed.

I laughed. "No. I mean, yes, you may kiss me."

"Oh." His lips quirked into a smile before he joined our lips. I waited for the sensory rush of emotion, some sign that I could erase what had transpired between Eric and me. It never came.

When we parted, Graham brushed his knuckles against my cheek. "That was nice," he said.

"Yes," I replied. It was nice; but it didn't make me feel extraordinarily special. I was still mousy Meredith—not a woman in love.

We parted with the promise of a picnic the next afternoon. I convinced myself to look forward to it. Graham was fun to be with, amusing, the perfect gentleman. I could be content with that. Couldn't I?

I had always avoided serious entanglements, preferring to play out a romance in written words. The arrangement had suited me—thus far. But lately, I, too, had longed for something novel, something magical.

Graham was different from the few men who braved interest in me. He was thoughtful, witty. I could always count on Graham to say nice things. Then why did I have misgivings about the course our relationship was taking?

All this deliberating made the knot at the back of my head begin to throb. I needed to be far away from my cumbersome thoughts. The large four-poster beckoned me to seek its protection. I crawled under the heavy blanket and sought relief. I fell asleep before my head hit the pillow.

Madelaine was waiting for me …

Overhead the massive chandelier sparkled against the candlelight. Laughter and merriment came from every corner of the room. A note of introduction sounded before the orchestra struck a lively waltz. Ladies and gentleman came together for the first dance at the event of the year: the Halloween masquerade ball.

Madelaine looked resplendent in a deep cut gown of gold lamè. The rhinestone mask and tall powdered wig could not hide her beauty. Marie Antoinette could not have looked as breathtaking. Many leers and admiring stares followed her around the room, but she had eyes only for her husband.

Edmund cut a dashing figure as a fifteenth century French nobleman. He led her proudly onto the dance floor. Her long skirts swayed to the melody. She felt wanted and needed in his arms. The dance was a ray of hope, the chance that things would be different now. Maybe Madelaine would have the marriage and children she always hoped to have; that the last months were only a dream, just a bad dream.

But with the return of the sun came the return of Edmund's indifference. His mood was once again quiet and sullen, leaving Madelaine filled with despair. It was a crushing blow after such a promising evening.

The dream did nothing more than confirm my suspicions that Edmund Boothe was a ruthless, hateful man. It did little to ease my concern over the curiosity I had for his son.

I went to my desk to scribble some notes while the dream

was still fresh in my memory. There was a respectable stack of manuscript pages accumulating. My story was beginning to take shape, or I should say Madelaine's story, for she had inspired each word. I had been given a rare opportunity to see life through an extraordinary woman's eyes. Why I was chosen for such a special gift, I did not know. There had to be a rhyme and reason to all of this. Exposing her life had a purpose more than just a plot for my book. I hoped there would be a happy ending for both.

It was still relatively early when I found myself alone in the dining room. Graham had yet to make an appearance. By the looks of breakfast, Linnea had been up and busy for some time. The peppered eggs were cold and leathery. I passed up the dish for a safer bite of a biscuit.

Graham was his usual merry self when he finally came down, dressed in canvas slacks and cotton shirt, ready for a day's work. "Good Morning," he bade as he entered the dining room. "It does one good to start the day off with such beauty to look at."

Always a nice word, that was Graham. "Good morning," I replied. "You look ready to start on a big project."

"I am. There are a few steps that need to be replaced on the rear staircase. It should take me a good part of the day."

Wonderful! I was anxious to get back to Madelaine's journal. "What about our picnic?"

"I think I could manage to spare a few hours for such a lovely lady. I'll have Linnea fix us something special. I might even be able to persuade her into making a pie."

As if on cue, Linnea walked in carrying a plate heaping with a steamy breakfast and placed it before Graham.

"Why haven't you eaten?" he asked, seeing my untouched plate.

"I lost my appetite."

"Well, no wonder," he said, examining my eggs, "you've let them grow cold."

Yes, no wonder. "If you'll excuse me," I said, "I have work of my own to do. A book won't write itself you know."

"That reminds me. I haven't heard one of your stories yet, at least not completely," he said sheepishly. "What if you brought one along on our picnic? You can read it to me. And I promise not to fall asleep."

"If you'd like."

Pausing only briefly in his assault of his plate, he nodded, his head snapping in approval. I went upstairs and crept into Graham's now vacant room. The journal sat in the drawer waiting patiently for me.

❧ TEN ❧

December 10

I helped Sarah prepare the nursery today. Her time is coming soon and she's getting anxious. I am too for that matter. She has been busy knitting and sewing all manner of little clothes. It's a wonder a person can fit into something so small. In turn, Sarah is helping me with a smoking jacket for Edmund. It will be his Christmas present. I hope it pleases him. I haven't been able to please him much lately.

December 25

Christmas Day. We went to services this morning held in the little chapel. I was pleased Edmund decided to attend after all. I wore the ruby broach he gave me. It was a very nice gift and very expensive. It was so nice I was almost ashamed to give him the handmade jacket. He was genuinely pleased with it and thanked me for the present even though it wasn't the son he had been hoping for. I wished it had been.

December 31

I found out I am not a drinking woman. I had always declined partaking in Edmund's brandy, but after failing in my attempts to make him happy these

94

past weeks I decided to give it a try. It was strong and bitter. I was sick for three days, unable to leave my bed. He said it would be good for me, that it took time to get accustomed to, but in the end it would assure a prolonged life. All I know is if I ever drink that elixir again it will assure the opposite.

January 5

I have sufficiently recovered, vowing never to drink spirits again. Edmund has left on business for two weeks and I am now alone. I know it is wrong of me to admit it, but I am relieved.

January 10

Jonathan has come into the world! Sarah has a son. Ian came for me late last night. When I got to Sarah's bedside she was in full labor. I stayed with her while Ian ran to fetch the doctor. It was the most frightening and wonderful experience. Jonathan is the most beautiful baby. I wonder if I will ever have one as beautiful.

February 3

The recent snowfall has hindered any hopes of visiting Sarah and the baby. She sent me a note detailing the progress of Ian's diapering attempts. He had it almost mastered but for a few accidents that left both Ian and son drenched. Somehow I could not see Edmund in that role.

March 22

The first buds of spring have sprouted. I'm anxious to transfer the seedlings I've started in the greenhouse to the garden. It will be some time, though, before the ground is ready. Sarah has some oregano and basil I would like to try. I thought I would put in a spice garden by the stables. I'll have to remember to ask Edmund about it when he comes back.

March 25

Edmund and I had a terrible row last night. I merely suggested clearing a spot for my spice garden when he became quite upset. All I would be harming is a detestable patch of unsightly hemlock. The hemlock is all but gone from these parts, he said. Good riddance is what I said. Sometimes I think he just refuses me as a punishment.

April 29

It has been a busy spring for the farmers. I watched little Jonathan for Sarah while she helped Ian with the shearing. He was so fascinated with the baby lambs frolicking in the pasture with their mamas. It seems all of Hemlock is brimming with new life. I wish I could play a part.

May 18

It has been a year since our marriage began. (Only one year?) And today I have found I am still without child. I have had ample time to conceive. Edmund has said as much. I've tried everything. Is there no hope for me?

I could see where a droplet of water, a tear, must have fallen on the word "hope" making the ink fan to a blur. I could feel my own tears welling up inside for Madelaine's plight.

How will I tell him?

May 20

The swelling on my cheek is still visible. I can't let Sarah see me like this. She will ask questions and I don't want her to think ill of Edmund. It wasn't his fault. I had promised him an heir and I failed him.

May 27

The pain in my cheek is gone but the pain in my heart grows. A small part of me died that night, the part that looked up to and trusted the man I married.

We've built a wall around ourselves to keep a distance from each other. I've accepted my circumstances for what they are, and I'm through trying to make Edmund different from what he is. Maybe now I can find contentment.

I wiped a lone tear from my cheek. "If Edmund Boothe were alive today ..." I cursed to myself. A bureau drawer rolled shut with a bang. I jumped with a start nearly toppling the bedside table. Blast! That little woman was sneaky. "Can I help you, Ana?" I asked while shoving the journal back into the drawer.

"No miss, I was just putting Mr. Ferguson's shirts away."

And hoping to catch me in the act again as well. Had she been lurking in the halls waiting for me to enter Graham's room?

"I'm sorry if I disturbed your ... reading," she sniffed.

"That's quite all right. I was just about to come looking for you," I said.

"For me, Miss?"

"Yes. I thought I would render my services again to help make Boothe House presentable. I'm sure you could use the help. Just point me in the right direction and I'll get started." A little bribery wouldn't hurt if it would ensure her silence. But then, I was sure that was what she had in mind all along.

"I couldn't ask you to do that. It's quite a job for me alone, what with all the mending and floors to scrub—"

"I insist," I said through clenched teeth. Next she would have me groveling at her feet.

"What would Mr. Ferguson say?"

"Don't worry about Graham. I'll assure him it's in his best interest."

"Well, the first floor has yet to be started. The fireplaces need to be swept out and the windows washed—" She stopped then and frowned. "It might be too much for a delicate woman like you."

I had underestimated the little housekeeper. She had to be admired for her manipulative tactics. "You can believe me, Ana, when I say my fainting the other day was merely a fluke. I'm quite healthy but for maybe the bump on my head. But it's nearly gone now and I feel fine. I have taken care of my father's house for over ten years so a little dirt will not hurt me."

There's a little and then there's a lot. After changing into more suitable clothing I started in the formal sitting room. I noticed some dirt on my first tour with Graham, but under closer inspection I found a mountain of it. There were cobwebs the size of small trees hanging in the corners and under the furniture. Layers of smoke and dust topped the tables and mantel. The fireplace looked to have been used a hundred times but never emptied. A mound of ash rose toward the chimney spilling out onto the marble hearth.

I brushed off the picture of Ignacious Boothe over the mantel first. It was an odd portrait of a graying man with a mocking smile and laughter in his eyes. I wondered what was going through his mind—or minds; he looked to have possessed several.

It mattered little it was daylight. I lit every lamp in the room. The spindly cobwebs and the way the portrait's eyes followed me around the room gave me the shivers. I threw every curtain and shade open, turned up every lamp, leaving no doubt as to what lurked in the shadows.

After I lined the empty wood box with newspaper, I grabbed my dustpan, and shovel upon shovel, filled the wood box with charred splinters and ash. The billowing dust I dislodged clogged my nose and throat making me cough. I reached up to open the damper to let some of the dust escape up the chimney. Like everything else in the house it was rusted shut. I needed a little leverage.

With the handle of the dustpan resting squarely in the eye of the damper handle and my weight centered underneath, I pulled, cursing and groaning with all my might. "For the love of—"

The damper gave way and so did my dust pan. I slid and fell face first into the fireplace. Stones and twigs pelted my head. Soot and debris covered my head and neck. I could smell it. I could feel it, even under the scarf tied around my head. And worst of all, I could taste it. I thought back to my evening gown and the admiring looks Eric and Graham gave me. If they could only see me now, I laughed, elbow deep in a pile of soot with my back end protruding from the fireplace. Thank heavens Graham was at the other end of the house.

"I don't believe we've met. Cinderella isn't it?"

Please no! I pleaded with any higher order that would listen. As luck would have it, no one was listening. I knew that voice and knew it well. The hard shell and mocking tone never ceased to have an effect on me.

Eric had returned.

Mortification was too mild a word. Nothing from my most hideous nightmare could compare to this. The damper was open. It looked wide enough. *Maybe if I could just crawl up the chimney and ...*

"You'll never make it." Eric read my mind. "You'll get stuck about half way up. I'll have a devil of a time trying to get you out, not to mention, ruining a perfectly good suit."

There was no escaping it now. With dread, I looked back over my shoulder to find him down on his haunches smiling. Why did he have to come back today, right now, looking so handsome, so … clean?

"Do you always spy on people?" I asked in irritation.

"I wasn't spying. I was merely walking in the door when I heard a barrage of curses. I didn't realize you possessed such a colorful vocabulary."

My palette had only just begun.

"Are you going to come out of there or do you plan on spending the rest of the day wallowing in ashes?" he inquired.

"I was hoping maybe you'd go away."

"Not likely. At least, not until you tell me what you're doing in there. Can't find your glass slipper?"

"You know how slippery glass is. I'm forever leaving it behind," I said, backing out of the fireplace carrying a heaping pile of cinders with me. A section of broken glass, the size of a petite shoe rolled out. I lifted it with a shrug. "Posh! The wrong size." I discarded the glass in the trash pile.

"Giving up already?" he challenged. "You don't strike me as the quitting type."

He was trying to goad me into a sparring match. Sitting on the floor with soot covering me from head to toe, I was hardly armed for battle. A wise woman knew when to retreat.

Eric refused to accept my surrender, however. "Tell me. Was it just odd curiosity that sent you into the fireplace or did you have a specific task in mind?"

"I was trying to help Ana. She can't be expected to have this entire house ready in time for the ball."

"No, she can't," Eric agreed. "That's why I've hired extra help. They start first thing tomorrow."

"You mean I've done all this—for nothing?"

"I wouldn't say it was for nothing. I found it quite amusing."

That was the final blow. Eric's tailored grey suit was looking much too clean for my comfort. "Would you help me up, please?"

"Yes, of course." He extended his hand to me then wrinkled his nose when my blackened hand took his. As he pulled me up I stumbled, falling flat against his chest marring his spotless clothes. He arched one eyebrow in surprise. "You did that on purpose."

"Yes, I did," I confessed, brushing off his lapel and adding more dirt in the process. "You deserved it."

"You know, Miss Barlow, you should be careful at how you throw yourself at a man. He may get the wrong idea."

"And what idea might that be, my lord?"

"Oh, something like this." His hands circled my waist, pulling me closer until my arms were pinned to his chest. He felt solid and strong. I knew I was in trouble. The heat from his embrace, the scent of clean soap on his skin, added more fuel to the fire now licking up my spine.

A lock of ebony hair fell to his brow as he tilted his head down just short of a kiss away. In a slow exhale of breath he whispered, "Or do you have more in mind?"

Could he read my thoughts, too?

The slight twitch at the corner of his mouth gave him away. I had walked into his little trap like an innocent lamb to slaughter. Squirming for release, I begged, "Please!"

"I'm sorry, Miss Barlow. You can plead all you want but I'm not going to ravish you."

"Oh! Of all the insufferable …" I pushed against the flat plain of his chest and broke free. "I'd just like to see you try!"

His grin was deliberately smug. "Yes, I believe you would."

"Ooh!" A tall brass candlestick stood on a round table next to the sofa and well within reach.

He sensed my intent and turned with a chuckle, leaving me gaping in his wake.

The man was truly insufferable. The most loathsome, detestable creature I had ever had the misfortune to meet. Then why could I not get him out of my bloody head?

One always had to be on guard with a man like Eric Boothe. It was a lesson I had temporarily forgotten. I looked down at my ash-covered limbs, soiled clothes and groaned. Was there no hope for me?

If I hadn't known better, I would have sworn I heard laughter coming from the painting over the fireplace. I glared up at the mocking of portrait of Ignacious Boothe. "Oh, shut up!"

"Well," I sighed. There was only one thing left to make my humiliation complete.

"Meredith, are you ready for our picnic?"

And that was Graham.

By the time I had bathed and changed, Graham had eaten all of the sandwiches and half of the pear pie. All that was left was an apple and a wedge of cheese. I took them before they too found their way into Graham's gullet.

We found a nice place by the lake near two silver maple trees. Their crimson and gold leaves had fallen to the ground making a soft cushion for our blanket. Graham settled himself in a recumbent position, his hunger fully sated.

I closed my wrap about me and began to read aloud the same story that had put Graham to sleep. When I had finished I put the book down and waited for the criticism to fall.

"Meredith, that had to be the most wonderful story I've ever heard."

It wasn't that good.

"What a talent you have," he remarked.

"You didn't think it at all … trite?"

"No, on the contrary, you kept me guessing all the way to the end."

"And the part where Alice runs into Peter in the park?"

"Wonderful!" he gushed. "I was completely baffled."

So was I. There was no Peter or Alice, and there was no park. Though I liked to hear Graham's glowing praise, I appreciated Eric's opinions more. Even if they weren't as flattering, they were honest. "That's enough about my story," I said, pushing my book aside. I had been insulted enough for one day. "I hear there's going to be a Halloween festival in the village this weekend. What type of costume are you going to wear?"

"Oh, I don't go to those things." He picked at the grass scrutinizing each blade.

"You don't? Why not? It sounds like fun. I think I'm going. If I can find some peasant clothes, that is."

"You could probably find something in the attic. There's all sorts of things up there."

"Really? Will you show me?"

"Madame, your wish is my command. Come."

We gathered our picnic basket and blanket and went back to the house. The attic was up over the ballroom, a dizzying height as I looked out the small oval windows. There was a treasure trove of interesting artifacts. I especially liked the wooden rocking horse. *Eric's?* Perhaps it left a splinter in a delicate area. No, that would be too much to hope for.

There were paintings of Boothe ancestors and landscapes. "What is this?" I asked, holding up a picture resembling Boothe House.

"Oh, that's Boothe House as it looked when it was first built. My great-grandfather built on to the place as it is today," Graham said.

It was a nice house, not as dark and menacing as the structure looked now. But who knew? After a good cleaning and some repairs it could recapture its appeal.

"Here we go," Graham said, locating a stack of trunks in the corner. "You take this one." He lifted the top one and placed it at my feet.

It was full of servant uniforms, and right on top was a plain grey scullery dress. With a few accents it would be perfect for the festival. I sifted through more of the clothes, some of them dating back a hundred years. There were some well-worn trousers with suspenders, a few flannel shirts and a wide brimmed hat. "I think these will fit you." I held them up to Graham for inspection.

"Meredith, I don't think this—"

"They'll fit perfectly. There's no reason for you not to go now."

"Maybe only one. I'm not welcome."

"Not welcome?" I remembered the cold stares and brooding suspicion I received when I first came to Hemlock, but I was a stranger and Graham had lived here most of his life. "Why not?"

"They never seem comfortable around me."

"Have you ever tried to make them feel otherwise?"

He shrugged. "Well, no."

"Then I wouldn't blame them. You have to give in order to receive. They're rather nice people once you get to know them."

"Oh? And how well do you know them?"

"Not very, but they're coming around. The festival is the perfect opportunity for you to blend in. We can make a mask for you if you'd like. That way no one will recognize you."

"If you insist."

"I do."

He gave an exasperated sigh, "Ah, the things I do for love."

"Graham—"

"Don't fret Meredith. There's no harm in hoping. Besides, I'll have you falling in love with me in no time. Just you wait and see."

He had determination—I gave him that. "What's in there?" I pointed to the other trunk.

"Oh, just some of Aunt Madelaine's things."

My eyes lit up at the mere mention of her. "May I look?"

"Be my guest," Graham offered.

When I opened it I couldn't believe my eyes. The material was a rich, indigo satin. French lace layered a veil around the bodice. It was a gown to take one's breath away. And underclothes. "Why they're beautiful!"

"I don't know why we kept them," Graham said with distaste. "Should have burned them a long time ago."

"You can't! It would be a sin."

"You're welcome to them. I have no use for them."

"What about Eric?" I wondered.

"I don't think they would fit him either."

I gave him a chiding look.

"But then again, blue is his color," he jested.

"Graham, stop," I scolded lightly. "The only person they would look good on is me."

"Then by all means take them. They might not be in fashion anymore, though."

"Oh, this style never goes out of date," I said, admiring the cut of each dress. There were everyday dresses that might have been a bit old fashioned, but the elegant evening gowns were perfect. My hopes rose when I thought of one in particular. I searched through the trunk load looking for that one dress. And there it was, at the bottom wrapped in blue paper, the gold Marie Antoinette costume. I now knew exactly what I was going to wear to the masquerade ball.

The dampened wig sat perched on the mantel resting over the clock. I had washed the years of yellowing away and reshaped it to dry. Its mate, the elaborate eighteenth century style gown lay over the corner chair. I could hardly contain my excitement. Finding the dress Madelaine had worn was a dream come true— literally. I only hoped I would do it justice.

The hour had grown late, and I had yet to dress for dinner. The prospect of seeing Eric again preyed on my nerves. After the mortifying experience he put me through that afternoon it would be understandable if I stayed in my room refusing to be anywhere near that intolerable man. But I was a glutton for punishment. Never let an adversary know your weakness or he will use it against you, the Colonel always said. Eric would not find me so vulnerable again. The soot was gone. The grass in my hair was gone. I was clean from head to foot. And I had the indigo evening gown.

I glided down the stairs, my head held high in confidence. It was amazing what a beautiful dress will do to you. I felt assured, in control and ready for battle. Then why was I trembling?

It was early yet. No one had come down. There was still time before the inevitable. I sought refuge in the library to collect my thoughts and warm my bare arms. The gown was exquisite in style but left much to be desired for warmth. As I held out my palms to the fire I looked up at Madelaine's portrait. I now knew the meaning behind the sadness in her eyes. What a sorrowful situation it all was. I counted myself lucky not to be in such dire circumstances, nor would I allow myself ever to be.

The library was a soothing place. It was the only other room in the house besides my garden room in which I felt comfortable. I noticed the cover over the piano had been removed. Unable to resist temptation, I ran my fingers over the smooth ivory keys. My father had kept my mother's old upright, but I seldom played it anymore. I sifted through the pile of music, many of them my favorites, and found *Liebestraum,* my mother's song. The notes looked familiar. I could almost hear the gentle sweep of the melody as she played it over and over. I sat on the bench and hoped the four years of study would come back to me.

The action of the grand piano was light and easy, the resonance sharply in tune. Unfortunately my playing wasn't. My fingers felt stiff and unpracticed, and it showed. My old piano tutor, Mrs. Cruthers, would be clutching her palpitating heart in horror if she heard me, I thought. With a cringe and a sharp that should have been a flat I finished. I did it. I played the piece through its entirety. Maybe butchered would be a better word for it, but I did it and enjoyed it, too. It helped me to relax. My nerves were no longer tied up in knots. With a little practice I could have it mastered, I mused. All right, maybe with a lot of practice—maybe.

"Bravo!" called a voice from the entrance to the library.

I should have known it would happen. If anyone were going to witness my defilement of beautiful music it would be Eric

Boothe. He walked straight and tall, looking especially dapper in a fine fitting black suit and crisp white shirt that matched his dazzling smile. I pictured him strolling into a courtroom in just that way and imagined the spectators admiring his striking good looks and sanguine presence—most of the women. I, myself, was not immune to them.

"Please tell me you didn't hear that."

"I wish I could say I didn't, but I did." He chuckled. "Don't worry. I won't tell anyone."

He didn't have to. I was embarrassed enough for a hundred witnesses.

"You have a knack for catching me at a disadvantage," I said with irritation.

"Does that bother you?"

"Yes!"

"Would it make you feel better if I promise to walk the other way the next time you are … at a disadvantage?"

"You won't have to," I said with conviction. "From now on there will be no disadvantage."

"That sounds like a challenge."

I scoffed, "I suppose you never get embarrassed?"

He shook his head. "I don't see any cause to."

"Not ever?"

He deliberated for a moment then leaned over the piano closing the space between us. "I'll let you in on a little secret. There was one occasion, my first case in open court. I was defending a man accused of illegal gambling. The first half of the trial went better than I anticipated. I had overshadowed every argument from the prosecution. I had the court eating out of my hands. That made me a bit overconfident, I guess, a little too cocky. I let my concentration slip. I thought I had the whole case sewn up, you see. Anyway, my notes got mixed up and I insinuated to the wrong witness she was lacking morals, was loose and had the credibility of a guttersnipe. It wasn't until I bothered to take a good look at the sixty-year-old woman foaming at the mouth from my atrocious accusations that I realized my error. Instead of grilling a young woman of ill repute like I thought I was, I had just questioned the reputation of the local school mistress and revered member of the church."

I couldn't imagine anything so horrendous. If I had suffered similar circumstances I would have crumbled into a million pieces right there on the spot. "Whatever did you do?"

"I made my apologies to the woman, the court and my client who was ready to fire me on the spot. I talked him out of it and managed to regain my concentration to finish the trial. Then, after it was all over, I went back to my office and drank myself numb."

We both laughed. My previous humiliations didn't seem so serious anymore. "Did you win your case?"

"Of course," he replied smugly.

I should have known. No one but Eric Boothe could foul so in error then end victorious. He started and finished with the upper hand. Whatever happened in between was of little consequence.

"Meredith, I hope I haven't scared you off. Feel free to play this piano whenever you like. I promise not to bother you. Whether you believe it or not I enjoyed hearing it again. It hasn't been played since my mother was alive."

There was a softness in his features and hope in his eyes, a wishing for things that had once been. He was doing it again, making me think he was almost human.

"I hate to see such an instrument go to waste," he added.

I doubted very seriously my playing was anything but painful to his ears. "Do you know what you're asking? In my hands this piano could become a lethal weapon."

He laughed, a deep rich sound that warmed my skin like tropical heat. Yes, he was doing it again. "You just need to practice."

"I think I'll stick to writing," I decided. "Pianos and fireplaces are not my calling."

Rising to put the music away, I stopped short at the look

on Eric's face. I could feel each movement of his eyes as they lingered on my dress—first on the bodice; then down each fold of the satin skirt. From wrist to ankle, tiny bumps rose on my skin. Did he recognize it? Would he despise me for conjuring the memory of his mother?

As I was about to beg his forgiveness, the grim set of his lips widened to a slow lazy grin. "You're giving a man ideas again, Meredith."

✂ ELEVEN ✄

It was those ideas that got me into trouble the last time. Having the advantage suddenly thrown into my lap was a little frightening. But I liked it. "Sorry, my lord. You had your chance." I headed to the dining room before he could see my smile of triumph. Eric's laugh followed close behind.

Graham was timely for a change. His entrance put an immediate damper on the amiable atmosphere Eric and I were sharing, but I would not allow it to hinder my enjoyment. I was too happy reveling in the throes of victory to let their rivalry interfere with my evening. And supper looked most promising.

We started in relative silence. The hot oyster bisque was a delicious treat for me. I seldom I had it, only when dining at Masion de la Mer, a quaint little French restaurant on the port whose bisque compared to none. Linnea's creation even rivaled that.

One good thing about Eric's return was finally having a decent meal. Linnea was on her best behavior when he was around. It still didn't keep me from eyeing my food suspiciously. The main course was, to my delight, stuffed veal breast, a favorite dish of mine. It looked and smelled irresistible. That was why I was cautious enough to poke it with my fork and underneath the parsley garnish for an ambush ready to strike when I least expected it.

"Looking for something?" Eric asked.

I looked up to find him eyeing me curiously. I wasn't about

to divulge my paranoia. "I can't seem to find my glass slipper."

He smiled. "I hope it turns up in time for the ball."

"So do I."

"What's this?" Graham wondered, just now entering the conversation. "Your slippers are missing?"

I shook my head. "No, it's nothing," I assured him. It was a private joke between Eric and me and for reasons beyond my ken I wanted to keep it that way. "Were you able to finish the stairs?"

"Mm, hmm. Of course, if I had known Eric had splurged and hired help I would have been spared the labor and had more time for our picnic, which by the way, I enjoyed immensely."

With Eric's attention on full alert, I couldn't bring myself to say, "me too." Was it a flicker of jealousy I saw in his expression?

"Yes, we've all been working our fingers to the bone." Graham gave Eric a disgruntled look. "Even Meredith here pitched in to help."

"I know. When I walked in she was busy up to her elbows."

Eric and I exchanged glances.

"By the way," he continued, "that wasn't what I had in mind when I asked for your assistance. I was thinking more on the lines of what to serve and how to orchestrate the whole affair."

"I do have a few ideas on that," I said.

Graham lifted his face away from his plate. "You do?"

I nodded, taking only a slight offense at his surprise.

"Let's hear them," prodded Eric.

"Well," I began, only too pleased to offer my brilliant suggestions. "As long as you've asked ..."

I had a great many ideas: hors d'oeuvres and foods from around the world, molded and shaped into a representation of their origins; ivy covered trellises in every corner of the dance floor and an orchestra, not large but with a few simple strings and harp. Small intimate tables set up around the perimeter of the room would allow the guests ample view of the room no matter where they sat. I could see it all so clearly: the ball

Madelaine had so meticulously planned herself. It had been hailed a success then and would be so again some thirty-odd years later. I outlined the event just as I remembered from my dream, sparing no detail.

"Sounds like you've given this a great deal of thought."

"Actually, it just came to me in a flash." Or something like that.

"It sounds costly to me," complained Graham. He had never kept his disapproval of the party secret. "I don't see how we'll manage."

"Don't look at it as a cost but as an investment," Eric said. "If it will help sell this house, as I think it will, the investment will be worthwhile."

That brought a frown to Graham's face. Whenever the subject of selling Boothe House was broached he retreated into a sulk.

"Besides," Eric added, "there's no turning back now. The invitations have already been posted. The ball will be held two weeks from this Saturday."

"What!" Graham sputtered.

The news flustered me too. Two weeks was a very short time, and there was so much to do. I couldn't blame Eric for wanting to be rid of this sinister abode and all its painful memories; but for Graham it held nothing but good memories. For the life of me, I couldn't figure out why, but that was something private for Graham.

Eric and I conferred on ideas and it seemed our minds were in league. I never thought it possible but we shared many of the same tastes. We even liked the same music. Working with him in an amiable atmosphere was a thrilling experience. I marveled at how fast and efficiently his mind worked. After finalizing the details I held little doubt we would indeed be ready in time for the ball.

Graham finally relented and offered his own suggestions. "We could award a prize for the best costume and maybe even enlist the guests in a game of pass the potato."

"Pass the potato?" I wondered aloud.

"It's where a potato is passed from one person to another down the line and the first line to bring it all the way to the end wins."

I looked at Graham curiously. "That doesn't sound too difficult."

He smiled that impish grin again. "It is if you don't use your hands."

That was the catch. A typical Graham game. Dare I ask? "Then how is it passed?"

"From chin to chin," he replied, then demonstrated. "You place the potato like so under your chin then pass it to the man or woman next to you and they catch it under their chin. Of course you make sure the men and women are staggered. It makes the game much more fun."

I could well imagine. It was bound to raise a few eyebrows. "It would certainly liven things up a bit."

Graham placed his hand over mine. "Especially if you're next to me."

I pulled my hand away pretending to adjust my napkin. Eric's witness to Graham's suggestive display made me uncomfortable.

"What do you say, Eric?" Graham asked.

The darker cousin laid his hands out in approval. "I leave the entertainment to you."

"As always," Graham replied. "I am the better man for the job eh, Eric?"

Eric lifted the corner of his mouth then sighed. "Yes, you are Graham. Whenever I need a good laugh I always think of you."

It took a full minute for Graham to understand the jibe for what it was. Unable to come up with a suitable reply, he slapped his jaws around a forkful of lemon meringue.

I pitied anyone who went up against Eric Boothe. He could turn the tables to his favor with the slightest effort. It made me wonder what he was capable of when he truly put his mind to a task.

The heavenly meringue was hard to leave. I had my fill and more. The sweet dessert was another delight of mine, and I made a mental note to express my enjoyment of the entire meal to Linnea. It would be a sharp thorn in her side, I thought with relish.

We moved to the library where Graham engaged me in a game of checkers. Naturally I won. Again and again. I was fairly certain he was throwing the games. At least, I thought he was. No one could be that obtuse. I tried to point out his error but he insisted I bested him fair and square.

He continued to hover over me possessively. There was the arm across my lower back as he guided me to the chair by the fire, the hand on my bare shoulder as he offered to fetch a wrap, and the suggestive references to our picnic and future ones. It was if he were branding me his property like an animal marking his territory.

It became annoying. With Eric as an audience, even more so. Ordinarily, I would have welcomed such flattering attention, but I worried Eric would get the wrong impression. I liked Graham and he was fun to be with, but to pursue anything further was still a question that was heavy on my mind. Now with Eric's return and the ever changing feelings he evoked in me the question grew even heavier.

"Meredith?" His subtle voice woke me from my reverie. Eric stood close, his arm resting casually on the mantel. My eyes darted to the spot where Graham had been and was no more. We were alone. "I wanted to tell you ..."

This was it. Just as I was beginning to enjoy our amiable truce he was going to become the demon again and control the advantage. It was just as well, I told myself. I had no business liking a man like Eric Boothe. He would eventually ruin what feelings I did have for him just like his father did to Madelaine. He even had the audacity to look me directly in the eye before he threw his disparaging remarks to throw me off balance.

"... thank you for staying on. I was hoping you would."

And off balance I went, but in the other direction.

His gentle smile warmed my skin. I tried to tell myself it was just the fire, but the longer I stared at his handsome visage the warmer I became. The words sounded sweet to my ears, like droplets of honey on sponge cake.

"I think you made the right decision," he said. "I'm only sorry you had to make it in the first place. I'm glad you did." He turned and flicked the stub of his cigarette into the fire. "And for Graham."

"For Graham?" I did not understand.

"He's been lonely up here for so long. I'm happy you two have struck up a … companionship."

The touch of regret in his voice made me want to reassure him otherwise. "But Graham and I—"

"Are well suited. I know," he replied. "Maybe he'll look toward the future now instead of the past. You'll be good for him, Meredith."

But not for you? Is that it?

"Here we are," Graham said, returning with a shawl. He placed it over my shoulders. I hadn't asked for one. Or had I? And, indeed, it had grown suddenly cold in the room.

"How about a game of poker?" Graham asked.

I shook my head. "I don't think so. It's been a long day. I think I'll just say good night."

"What about tomorrow? Another picnic?"

"That sounds lovely," I said. My eyes strayed to Eric, but his face was void of expression.

"I'll walk you to your door then," Graham offered.

"That's not necessary. I can manage. I'll see you tomorrow." I deliberately placed a kiss on Graham's cheek in front of Eric. I didn't know what I was hoping for. Revenge? A spark of jealousy? "Good night," I said to Graham, his eyes merry with triumph.

He kissed my hand. "Until tomorrow."

"Good night, Eric."

"Good night, Meredith," he answered solemnly. "Pleasant dreams."

When I closed my eyes that night, tucked snugly in the four-poster, pictures of Graham flooded my mind. Eric was right. I would be good for Graham and he for me, if being pampered and patronized appealed to me. There would be many picnics, laughter, an occasional decent meal. I'd be sure to win card games and checkers and receive wonderful praise for everything I said and did, and probably for things I didn't do. I would be content with such a life. Wouldn't I?

It would be a better life than with Eric, a better life than Madelaine had. Though there were many dissimilarities between Eric and his father, there were also many similarities. Eric had a power about him that drew people to him. He used that power for his own gain much like his father. Any woman would rue the day she fell in love with him.

True to his word, Eric's hired help arrived bright and early the following morning. The workmen began clearing the front of the house and within an hour had made a vast improvement. The tangled vines and withered brush had been removed, and casts were being made to replace the fallen mortar pieces.

Ana had a time of it trying to teach the new maids the lay of the house. Linnea was busy herself with her own assistant and in all her glory for having someone under her command. I could breathe a little easier knowing there was someone to witness Linnea's food preparations. For most of the morning, I stayed to myself, out of everyone's way. There were a few stolen moments when I was able to sneak into Graham's room to read Madelaine's journal.

They had fallen into a routine, Madelaine and Edmund. With no hope of having a child, she gave up trying to please Edmund and settled into her duties as the lady of the manor. In turn, Edmund ceased his pressuring and treated her with more respect than when they were first married. He would still claim his husbandly rights, more for need than hope of an heir. She would succumb to him as a dutiful wife should, but there was no passion anymore, no tenderness. The infatuation that had claimed them so quickly soured.

She tended to her garden with loving care, taking solace in watching the blooms flower and grow in place of the lifeless garden inside her womb. More than any woman, Madelaine desperately needed a child to love. If only Eric knew how much he was wanted and loved perhaps he would not be so bitter. I wanted so desperately to understand. Time for research was limited, however, to these few stolen moments of reading her journal. The answer was in there, I was certain. I just had to be patient.

The new maids bustled from bedroom to bedroom limiting my reading time. I returned to my room to find a surprise. On the bed lay an original copy of a novel by Agatha Christie, a marvelous author whom I admired immensely. Graham must have left it there in order to ease his conscience about lying to me before. I didn't remember mentioning Miss Christie to him but I must have, in passing, I supposed.

I began some creative writing myself. After several pages, I read over what I had written. The structure was well formed and the details outlined, but it seemed lacking. It seemed … trite. I needed advice from my most worthy critic, the Colonel, but the miles separating my father and I made that idea implausible. I could ask Graham. That was not a realistic solution either after his comments on my other book. No, there was only one person who might be able to help me. I would have to humble myself and swallow my pride. "I'd rather be harvesting manure," I grumbled, but there was no going around it. My writing needed help and he was the only one who could give it. Maybe he would refuse. Not likely. Eric would be only too happy to tell me what I did wrong.

I found him in the old barn that now housed motorcars and

various kinds of machinery. He was in the process of sorting tools and things for the rubbish pile. Though the air held an autumn chill, I noted he wore no overcoat. His sleeves were rolled up to his elbows and his collar unbuttoned exposing a shadow of dark hair. His lower arms had grease smudges where his muscles flexed, and his brow perspired from his heavy labor. I had to remind myself of the reason I was there, and it wasn't to ogle the man.

"Watch out!"

I jumped out of the way as two bicycles rolled out the entrance and landed at the base of the heap.

"You're not going to throw those out are you?" I asked him.

He pretended not to hear.

"They're still in good condition. You could at least sell them or something," I suggested. "And these garden tools. They're still good. The new owner may need them to restore the garden."

He threw a bundle of twisted wire on the pile and me a look of annoyance. "That's why I'm keeping the other ones. That pile is going to the Willowcrest."

The orphanage. "Oh," I said, and proceeded to mind my own business.

"Where's Graham?" he asked. "I thought you two were going on a picnic."

I shrugged. "We are but Graham is usually late."

"So you thought you'd come down here to supervise the cleaning of the barn?"

"No," I drawled back. "Actually, I came to ask for your opinion on my book." I didn't expect the swallowed pride to leave such an enormous lump in my throat.

He laughed outright.

"You're not going to make this easy are you?"

"You're serious, aren't you?"

I nodded, now dreading I ever considered him in the first place.

"I'm sorry," he replied in earnest. "What do you want to

know."

I deliberated turning around and heading back to the house but he seemed contrite enough, and I couldn't bring myself to leave his company. "You said my stories were trite."

"I also said they were good overall," he added.

"But what didn't you like about them? What did I do wrong?"

"Well, in *Invitation to a Crime,* besides the fact that it was predictable, your crime was too logical."

"It's supposed to be a love story."

His lips curved seductively. "That part was not trite at all."

The temperature under my collar rose significantly. "Then what part was?"

He tossed another bundle of wire onto the pile. "Your jewelry theft. I knew precisely what was going to happen and who was going to do it by the time the dinner was over."

"But how could you? Robert didn't steal the necklace until the next day."

"It was obvious. He needed the money. He was the favored and spoiled son."

"His brother Michael had just as much excuse," I argued. "He was cast out. He was—"

"Do you want my opinion or not?"

I clamped my mouth shut. "Go on."

"In every mystery there is an element of surprise. Yours was minimal. Your idea of the perfect crime was realistically far from perfect."

"And I suppose you know just how to commit the perfect crime?"

He smiled that know-it-all grin. "The perfect crime is one that looks as if no crime was committed at all. Now if you had Robert replace the priceless gems and antiques with counterfeits no one would have known he took them."

His logic escaped me. "Then how could he frame Michael to make the family shun him more?"

"He doesn't have to. At the beginning of the story you could have Michael fall upon a bank report or something that made him suspect Robert was up to something. The burden of proof and the mystery to what he did would have rested on Michael. Play upon their strengths—and their weaknesses. Everyone has at least one."

"Oh? And what's yours?" I wondered. "Outside of orphaned children."

"That, my dear Meredith, will remain my little secret."

"Hmm." *And what I wouldn't give to learn that one.*

He did have a good point, though. My story was too straightforward. The how and why was spelled out too quickly. "You'd make a good barrister, you know that?"

"So they tell me."

I liked his smile. "I always thought barristers were stuffy, old, bald men who pointed and accused everyone who crossed their paths."

"And now?"

"I still think they're stuffy, old, bald men who point and accuse everyone—"

He advanced on me before I had a chance to finish. "Care to take that back?"

I backed away from him into the barn. There was a wall on either side of me blocking any escape. What else could I do? "All right! I take it back. You're not bald."

He lunged toward me knocking into a shelf of gardening pots and tools. As pandemonium began falling down around us, I darted passed him out the door. The echo of pots crashing, tools clanging and angry cursing followed me across a meadow. I turned back in time to see Eric stumble from the barn. He looked in both directions before spotting me. I did what any self-respecting coward would do—I ran.

I skirted over a fallen tree and down toward the lake. I could hear Eric closing in breaking through the brush at a dangerous speed. Tall grass and thick bushes edged the shoreline. I ducked under the bough of a birch tree and kneeled behind a forsythia.

Eric came into view at the edge of the water. He walked within inches of my hiding spot and stepped out onto the dock, his chest heaving rapidly. My own heart thumped wildly in my chest. I covered a hand over my mouth to silence a giggle.

Eric raised his hand over his eyes to shield them from the glare off the water and looked around. Not finding his quarry, he gave up and trotted back toward the barn. I sighed with relief and a touch of regret. In some perversely idiotic way I wanted him to find me.

"Caught you!"

His hand caught me from behind, scaring the dickens out of me. I jumped to my feet with a scream knocking Eric off balance. He fell with a splash into the water, backside first.

Arms flailing, he came to the surface for air. "I …" His head went under the dark murky water a second time. He rose again to gulp another breath. "Can't … swim!"

He couldn't swim! *Dear God!* I watched him fight the water for each breath, choking, sputtering and was seized with panic. Eric was drowning and he was drifting further out.

"Hold on!" I yelled to him. I stripped off my shoes and raced onto the dock. *Please God, help me save him!* I jumped off the dock into the water and immediately hit the bottom. The water was only knee-high.

Eric's laughter carried over the water, up the hill and across the entire valley. He sat up out of the water and grinned.

"That wasn't funny," I replied, trying to remain serious but failing miserably. "The water is ice cold!"

"Yes, it is," he answered. "But it was worth every drop. Give me a hand, will you?"

I started to extend my hand then stopped. "Oh, no. You're not going to pull me in there."

"Meredith," he said rising from the water like Triton himself. His shirt was soaked nearly translucent and I could see every flex of muscle. Water fell in rivulets off the sturdy curve of his nose to his chin. And as he spoke in a soft coaxing voice, my toes curled deep into the sand. "If I had wanted to get you wet. I would have done this—"

In one swift movement, he lifted me off my feet and slung me over his shoulder. "Don't you dare!" I cried.

"I never dare, Meredith. I act." He turned from shore and walked steadily into deeper water.

Cold moisture seeped from his clothes through to my skin making me shiver. I pounded his back with my fists. "Eric Boothe, you put me down this instant!"

"I intend to."

"No! I mean on dry lan—"

Water rushed over my head like a tidal wave. It was cold, wet and invitingly stimulating. I thrashed about trying to find my footing. Eric seized my arm and pulled me up to his chest. "You don't know how to swim, do you?" he asked.

"Not particularly," I replied, feeling the warmth from his body and reveling in it.

"And *you* were going to save *me*?" He laughed.

"Actually," I drawled. "My plan was to hold you under."

"That does it!" With a chuckle, Eric lifted me up and threw me toward shallow water. I landed with a shriek and a giggle. When I came to my feet I wagged a finger at him. "This means war!" I began splashing at him, but his arms were longer and stronger. Wall upon wall of water came down on my head and arms. I could barely breathe. My side ached from laughter.

"Surrender?" he asked. His smile was arresting.

How easy it would be to give in to his demand, I thought. I decided then, that it was all right to like this man who fought like a lamb and played like a tiger. "Never!" I cried and dove for his midsection.

The blow hit him off guard. In a whoosh of breath, he fell backwards carrying me with him. We rolled to the surface, laughing. We were shallow enough where I could stand, but I didn't have to. Eric cradled me gently in his arms keeping my head well above water. My body shivered, but I did not feel cold.

"Your lips are blue," he said, his voice low and methodical.

"Are they?" I pressed my fingertips to my lips. They felt numb. "So are yours."

His eyes shifted with indecision. "Then what do you suppose we should do about it?"

Do about it? That was a dangerous question to ask a woman who liked the feel of his shoulders beneath her palms, who wanted to stroke his chin and explore the shallow cleft, and who remembered a certain kiss that melded every fantasy into one.

One corner of his mouth quirked upwards. "You're blushing, Meredith."

"Am I?" My hands covered my cheeks.

"You don't have to be embarrassed. I find it quite charming."

"I'm not embarrassed," I defended.

He laughed. "Then I suggest we get out of the water before I do something that will embarrass you—or cause you to catch pneumonia." He carried me to shore and set me carefully on my feet. I gathered my shoes and headed up the hill thinking about this new plateau our relationship had landed on and how easy it would be to tumble off the edge. Each step had to be a careful one.

We walked in relative silence until the squish and squeak of Eric's sodden shoes made us stop and look. Our eyes met, and we laughed anew. "You should have removed them before you went into the lake," I said.

"If I recall correctly, I wasn't given the option," he chortled.

By the time we reached the barn, Graham was there waiting for us. "What's going on here? Meredith, you're all wet. What about our picnic?"

I shrugged. The air was chilly and my teeth began to chatter. "E … Eric fell into the wa … water and I jumped in to save him." Just thinking about the entire scene made me giggle.

"Oh?" Graham raised a skeptical eyebrow. "Well you needn't have bothered. The man's a fish."

"So I noticed." I wiped the hair from my eyes and looked toward Eric. He leaned against the barn door pouring water out of his shoes. "It was sort of ... an accident."

"Well, you'd better go up and dry off if you want to go on the picnic. Linnea made lemon custard."

I would do just about anything for lemon custard. "I'll go change." I turned to Eric and smiled. "Thank you for your ... advice."

He cocked his head to one side to bat the water out of his ear. "My pleasure."

The picnic was pleasant. Graham ate most of the food and even managed to finish what I couldn't. I thanked him for the book. He seemed confused at first then said it was the least he could do.

I kept thinking of what would have happened down at the lake if I had followed my instincts and pressed my blue lips against Eric's. Would he have kissed me back? My imagination went into full throttle conjuring up images of flesh meeting flesh and entwined limbs. The depictions bordered on criminal.

"You're in the clouds, Meredith," Graham said, catching me staring off into a world of my own. "Thinking about your book?"

I turned with an apologetic smile. "Something like that," I replied. "I was just plotting my next crime."

≈ TWELVE ≈

Late into the evening, I fixed what I had written earlier. Eric's advice had truly helped. There was still plenty of mystery and surprise left for Madelaine's story because I was still much in the dark myself.

I wasn't given an opportunity to return to the journal, however, for another day. That left me pent up with curiosity. I roamed the house impressed with the changes taking place. Wallpaper was reglued and plaster repaired, draperies mended and rehung. The house was making an enormous transformation, yet there was still a feeling it was all a mirage. Behind the neatly refurbished walls lurked a legacy, listening and waiting, choosing its time to shatter the illusion and unleash its wrath. Boothe House would never really change. I still felt cold and unwanted as I walked the halls, or maybe it was just the reception I now received from Eric.

I hadn't spoken to him since the episode at the lake. He was quiet and reserved. There was a tension between us. The moment I stepped into the room I sensed it. This puzzled me. His eyes would not meet mine. In fact, he did not once look my way. Instead, he left the room as soon as Graham appeared. He even left the library when Graham and I entered together. It almost seemed as if he were more in favor of my relationship with Graham than before. The man was truly baffling. After our romp in the water I thought—oh, I don't know what I thought. Misguided delusions, I guessed.

There was a smile waiting for me from Graham, though. We worked on our costumes for the festival. The gardener clothes fit him well. I tried to convince him the mask hid too much of his handsome face, but he insisted on wearing it anyway.

He seemed almost anxious for the next evening. The festival would be fun, I assured him. I wondered if Eric were going, too.

"That would be the day," Graham guffawed. "My cousin is not the fun type. I don't think he knows how to be anything but serious."

Had it been a few weeks before, I would have agreed, but there was another side of Eric, Graham never saw. There was the time in the library, the time when he found me humiliating myself in the fireplace, and of course the lake. I smiled to myself. No, he was not serious all of the time.

"He's making remarkable progress on the house," I commented.

"Yes, he is," Graham remarked dryly. "Money makes all the difference."

"I'm sure he's keeping costs down as much as possible."

"He doesn't have to. He has plenty of it. What you don't understand, Meredith, is that when my uncle died he was a very rich man."

"But I thought—"

"That's what Eric wants everyone to think. He almost had me believing it too. He has it stashed away somewhere, I know it. I've been sweating away up here living on next to nothing while he sits on a gold mine. It is only now, when he wants to sell the place, we see it."

"I'm sure once Boothe house does sell you'll be amply included." I didn't know what else to say. If it all went to Eric it was his to do with as he chose. It seemed a bit selfish not to share it with your only living relative.

"It may not have to come to that." A smug ring entered Graham's voice.

"What do you mean?"

"I just may get to keep Boothe House after all."

"Graham ..." I narrowed my eyes. "What are you up to?"

He kissed my hand. "It's a surprise."

I was never more worried over a "surprise" in my life.

Eric was noticeably absent from supper. I had chosen another of Madelaine's gowns. It was deep emerald velvet and much warmer than the indigo, but the lines were just as sleek and hugged my curves comfortably. I took extra pains with my appearance that evening, but only Graham was there to notice.

The hammering, sawing and constant sound of voices vanished as work for the day ceased. We were left alone in relative silence. We played the usual games, but they held little enjoyment for me. There wasn't much of a challenge in knowing what the outcome would be. Like the old saying: winning isn't everything. Perhaps to Graham it was.

He wouldn't even give me a hint about his surprise. "You'll have to wait and see," he said. "It will secure our future." There was little consolation in that.

He held my hand as we sat by the fire. I waited for the rush of sensations to flow through my arm, but none came. I felt no longing desires, no skip of a heartbeat. His kiss did not leave me wanting more.

I went to bed that night wrestling with my thoughts. How could a man who worked so hard at trying to please me hold only a mild attraction, and yet, the man who cared little for my sensibilities take my breath away with only a glance? It didn't make sense.

I tossed and turned begging Madelaine to reveal an answer for me. The room grew cold as the fire withered. I rose to put the last two logs on the fire but found the woodbin empty. I was sure there were two there before. It didn't really matter. Two logs would not last long, anyway. I was just as far from sleep as I was hours before. There was ample wood in the library. An armful of choice logs would see me through the night or at least long enough to let sleep claim me.

The hall was dark and cold. The chill seeped right through the light silk of my gown. The eerie silence added another shiver to my already shaking flesh. Not a sound came but for a few creaks and groans of an old house settling against the wind; or an old ghost settling in for the night, I thought with a shudder.

The coals still glowed in the library fireplace. I stopped just long enough to wiggle my toes and warm my hands in front of it.

"You'll catch your death of cold roaming the house like that." Eric's voice was strained and quiet.

I clutched my heart and took a moment to catch my breath from the fright. "I'm sorry. I didn't know anyone was in here. I just came to get more wood for the fire in my room." My eyes adjusted to the darkness. I could see the outline of his form in the chair by the window. He sat motionless. I moved to gather some wood.

"Here," Eric said. "Let me help you."

"Do you always sit here in the dark?" I asked.

"It has its advantages."

I could feel blood rise from my neck to my cheeks. "We missed you at supper."

"Somehow I doubt that." He lifted a log and placed it in my arms.

I frowned. "We didn't see much of you all day."

"I was busy with the house. Unfortunately, I can't be everywhere at once."

"I was beginning to think you were trying to avoid me."

"Maybe I was." He lifted another log into my arms. The rough skin of his strong hand brushed against mine. I pulled back instinctively. The logs fell to the floor with a thud. "Don't," he said when I bent to retrieve them. He took a step forward and tilted my chin up with the crook of his finger. "I don't know what it is about you, Meredith. You've crept under my skin and

I'm not sure I like the feeling." His thumb led a lazy trail across my lips and back. "I've read all of your books. And do you know why I read them?"

I shook my head. I couldn't even begin to wonder.

"I read them because there's a little piece of you in each story. I hear your voice in the words and I can't put them down. Every night I lie awake wondering what it would be like to kiss you. I've wondered too long, Meredith."

"But you ... you already did kiss me. Remember?" His breath felt hot and liquid against my cheek. My nerves began to unravel at the ends.

"Yes, but this time I want it to mean something." His lips parted and gathered mine in a seductive dance.

If I had thought he was a master before, I was merely deluding myself. Now he proved beyond a shadow of a doubt there was no man on earth as skilled as he was. His chin was rough and unshaven. He kissed my lips, my brow, my cheek. The anticipation was shear torture.

"I thought you don't make molesting women a habit."

His breathing came deep and raspish. "I don't. But you're a hard habit to break." His hands cupped each side of my face to pull me closer and deeper inside of his kiss. I felt myself float in and out of a dream, the sensation so glorious my body threatened to break at the seams.

His voice became ragged as he pulled away. "I think we had better stop here before my habits turn corrupt."

My lips felt numb and swollen. "I—"

He placed a finger across my lips. "We can talk tomorrow. Right now I think you should go to bed." He lifted the logs back into my arms. "I don't think I can take much more of that light shining through your night dress."

I had acted like a woman of the world and now I blushed like a silly schoolgirl. When I got back to my room I dumped the logs in an unceremonious heap and fanned my face. Who needed a fire? It was as hot as blazes!

* * *

According to the mantel clock I had overslept and missed breakfast, a fact that didn't soothe my grumbling stomach any. It was well worth it, though. It took a great deal of effort to leave the wonderful comfort of Eric's arms in my dream. And it was not only a dream. It had happened, last night in the library. I had relived those magical moments over and over again in the bliss of slumber.

It was just a kiss, I scolded myself. They happen all the time, every day. Well, maybe not every day. A kiss like that only happened once in a lifetime. Hopefully twice. What was I saying? How quickly I had forgotten whom I was dealing with. Eric Boothe was not a man to be trusted. He caught me in a moment of weakness and I didn't doubt for a minute that he would use it against me.

Why couldn't it have been Graham, the considerate cousin, who plied me with kind words and gifts? Though Graham was far from perfect he was funny, predictable and madly in love with me. That was hardly cause to marry him, though. After having a taste of real passion I couldn't settle for second best. And wouldn't.

Voices raised in anger echoed along the hallway. They were at it again. I dressed quickly and sprung toward the stairs. Graham was whining like a child and Eric's patience had had enough of it. I halted on the steps. The library doors were closed, but I could still understand every word. And so could Linnea.

"Uh, hmm!" I cleared my throat.

She immediately straightened when she heard me. The reproachful look I sent her way had her stalking back to the kitchen with a crimped lip snort. There was no hope for a bite to eat now.

The row in the library calmed. There was just the murmur of sullen voices. I wanted very much to know what was going on in that room, but eavesdropping was beneath me—at least when there was a good chance of getting caught. Sneaking into someone's private quarters was a different matter entirely, and I took advantage of the opportunity.

In Madelaine's journal I hoped to find many answers. Why she had left was the first and foremost question. Curiosity about Eric held me too. He was the product of an unhappy union, and it was bound to affect the man today. I could see the cold ruthlessness of his father's upbringing, but lately there were shades of Madelaine in him.

Quietly, I closed the door to Graham's room. I removed the journal from the drawer and took my seat on the bed. It had become the pattern. I came to the place where I had hurriedly left off.

September 1

Edmund has informed me we will again host a masquerade. He has uncannily arranged it for the same night as the village festival. I shall have to miss the festival. I was so looking forward to it. Sarah will have to tell me all about it afterwards. There's always next year.

My days will be filled with preparations now. I'm glad for the distraction. The garden is breathing its last breath before winter. There is not much to do there anymore.

October 14

While Edmund is away on business I took a few hours to visit Sarah. It is remarkable how much Jonathan has grown since last I saw him. Has it really been a month? Sarah confided in me that she is almost certain there was another one on the way. I couldn't be happier for her. I don't envy her sickness though. With her morning nausea, Jonathan's activeness and her brother's upcoming visit she has her hands full. I promised her I would return soon to lend a hand.

November 1

Where do I begin? The ball went well, so I'm told. I didn't stay for its entirety. Edmund's barrister friends tired me with their legal talk so I left early to change into my costume for the festival. Edmund wouldn't miss me. My duties, welcoming guests and dancing the opening waltz were over. There was no reason he would need me for anything.

The bonfire rose high and so did my spirits as soon as I joined the fun. There was laughter and music. Everyone from the village was there and even several unfamiliar faces. I searched for Sarah and Ian but couldn't find them. I knew I should have kept trying and not have paid any attention to the man following me. He was harmless at first. A smile here and there, a jest or two that made me laugh. Oh, it felt so good to laugh! It was when he touched my hand to claim a dance that I knew I was lost. Though he wore a silly sheepskin mask, I could see he was handsome, as handsome as the devil. He may have been a stranger by name but not by heart. I felt I had known him a lifetime. He felt it too, and when he kissed me I came alive again.

When the rain came down on our heads we ran, hand in hand, into the woods for cover. We took shelter in the abandoned hunter's lodge.

I hadn't meant it to happen. But I'm not sorry. God may punish me for the sin I've committed and rightly so, but I'll never regret it. I've found true love. I've never been so happy and so sad in all my life!

I could feel her torment pouring from the page. If it hadn't been written in her own words, I never would have believed it. "There was another man!"

❧ THIRTEEN ❧

I couldn't pass any judgments on her, knowing what I did. Faced with a loveless marriage it was understandable she would seek affection elsewhere. My curiosity was in full swing. Who was he?

November 3

He asked to see me again. I couldn't. If Edmund found out he would be terribly angry. I fear the worst. My time with him may have been brief, but I love him with all my heart. He will be leaving Hemlock soon. I may never see him again.

November 5

A box was delivered today. In it was a small gold clock. It is the most beautiful clock I have ever seen. On the note he wrote: "I shall count the hours until we next meet." There was more. He asked me to meet him at the hunter's lodge.

I did.

November 7
He's gone. I think it is very possible to die from a broken heart.

November 25
Whenever I look at the clock I think of him. It ticks on relentlessly. Hours pass with my knowledge that I will never see him again. As I lay with Edmund it is he I am with. Will the pain never leave?

December 20
I have suspected for some time, but now I am most certain ...

The soft muffle of padded footsteps alerted me someone was coming. The accompanying whistle could be none other than Graham's. "Oh! For pity sake!" I slammed the book shut and threw it in the drawer. I blended behind the curtains as his foot crossed the threshold. I prayed he would not have a desire to view the scenery outside.

He turned toward the bed. The brandy on top of the bedside table was still swirling inside the decanter. My breath held silent as his eyes fixed on the table. He crossed the room and stood a mere few feet from where I stayed hidden. I cursed Graham for making me hide like this; I cursed Madelaine and Edmund for driving me to it; and I cursed myself for coming to this god-forsaken house in the first place.

His hand reached down and picked up a square gold cuff link from the table. He bounced it on the palm of his hand then strode from the room. "Ana?" he called. "I found one but where is the other?" His voice faded down the hall.

I exhaled. That was too close. But I was not out of danger yet. Graham was bound to return any moment. The table nearly toppled over in my haste to leave the room. I didn't slow until the door to my bedroom closed behind me.

My heart continued to race. That was too close indeed. Guilt, shame, remorse all ran through my mind. I hated playing such a devious role. It was terrible to take such advantage of Graham's trust and kindness. And for what? For some passages in a journal, written by a woman thrown into marital turmoil, who sought refuge in the arms of another man?

And I wouldn't rest until I went back there.

I was left dangling by a thread of suspense. What did Madelaine suspect? That Edmund found out about her? That she had some incurable disease? Once again, Graham's timing had been perfect.

The clock on the mantel chimed the hour. The clock. I knew it was the one he had given her. Small, intricate, given as a symbolic gesture to the women he loved. She treasured that piece and now I knew why. How long it had been ticking, in wait for them to be together again. Did Madelaine ever see him again? If rumors were correct, she did. But would she give up all to be with the man she thought she loved? How could she be sure? They had known each other just a scant time. How could she leave her son?

Passion was a powerful emotion. I knew first hand how controlling it could be. I had felt vulnerable and lost in Eric's arms, a feeling in which I didn't object. Not in the least. What I experienced was just a sampling of what passion could bring, and yet I understood how she felt. Would I have done the same as Madelaine? Would I have forsaken my vows for the comforting arms of another man? What if the other man were Eric?

In essence he was. Graham had been courting me and I had been letting him. There were no vows spoken, no promises given, but I still felt I had betrayed him. There was one difference between Madelaine's situation and my own: they had loved each other. I was not sure of my feelings for Eric. I was not sure of anything where he was concerned. I only knew that when we were together, emotions collided

My stomach rumbled on, only louder than before. I was

famished. I decided to go to the village to visit Aggie. Maybe I could beg a scone or two from her. I had promised to return there anyway to bring her up to date on the city news.

No one noticed as I crept out of the house. No one except Eric. He was outside surveying the repairs with the workmen. My heart took a sudden lurch when I saw him. He stopped and turned in my direction, but I couldn't face him. Not yet. The memory of his kiss was still too fresh to think rationally.

"Meredith! Wait!"

"Damn!" I cursed as I slammed the car door shut. Escape was nearly mine.

He leaned over the passenger's side. "Where are you going?"

"To the village. The festival is tonight so I thought I would lend a hand."

"I thought you might be leaving us for good."

"Not unless you want me to," I said cautiously.

He looked at me oddly. "No. We have a party to plan, remember?"

Of course, how could I forget? What other reason would he have for me to stay? "I thought everything was set."

"It is. I'll be right there!" he threw over his shoulder. "Will I see you tonight?"

I shook my head doubtfully. "There's the festival ..."

"I won't take too much of your time, but I think we need to talk." He looked so serious. Was he going to say it was all just a joke? That his feelings for me were more platonic than passionate?

"The festival doesn't begin until after dark. I should be back—"

"Good! I'll see you then."

Many possibilities ran through my mind as I pulled up to Croakers. There could be a number of reasons why he wanted to talk to me: the arrangement of flowers for the ball, the selection of music, the reason why our kiss was a mistake. Could I stand the rejection?

"Hello Aggie," I greeted as I entered the familiar pub.

"Meredith!" She waved. Duff even nodded in greeting.

"Are you ready for the festival tonight?" I asked.

"Oh, I've been baking up a storm. Would you like to try some of my apple bread?"

My stomach rumbled in response. "I thought you'd never ask."

We shared a pot of tea while I told her about my visit with Sarah. I left out my thoughts about Sarah hiding something. I knew whatever Sarah told me, she had told no one else.

The apple bread was delicious. I couldn't seem to get enough of it.

"Don't they feed you up there?" Aggie finally asked after watching me devour my third helping.

"Linnea was busy—"

Aggie dismissed the cook with a wave of her hand. "Don't get me started on that one. You just help yourself. There's plenty more. I make it every year for the festival."

I was relieved to hear that. I told her about the ball while I helped myself to another piece.

"So they're going to sell the place?" she mused.

"Try to anyway."

She shook her head. "I don't know. Who would want a place like that?"

"It's not so bad," I said. "They've already started fixing it up."

"It will take a lot more than fixing up to get rid of those demons. I'd keep an eye over my shoulder if I were you, it being Halloween and all."

I scoffed. Though I may have at times believed the rumors, I hadn't proved to myself I'd seen a ghost. My dreams could only be just that—dreams. The bump on my head had come, and gone and there hadn't been any further occurrences. Then again, I hadn't stepped foot in the master bedroom since. "Why do you suppose a spirit haunts?"

She shrugged. "Restless soul, I suspect. Unfinished business to attend to."

It made me wonder what unfinished business Edmund had.

"Can I get you some more?" Aggie inquired.

"Yes, please. At the rate I'm going there won't be any bread left for the festival."

"Don't you worry about that," said Aggie. "All the women in Hemlock bring something. There will be plenty to go around. Why, Sarah brings her brandied pears; Mildred, her mincemeat; Kate usually brings a chicken stew, and then there's the roast pig. Duff just put it on the fire."

It sounded wonderful. Wait until Graham sees all that food, I thought. I probably wouldn't see him for the rest of the night.

A man walked in. I recognized him as Charlie Pruitt, the father of Alicia Mae. He always wore a solemn expression. From what I had been told, he hadn't smiled since the day they found his daughter in the lake.

"You're back from town early, Charlie," Aggie said.

"I never made it that far. The wagon broke an axle," he said in disgust.

"Then you didn't get the candy goblin?"

Charlie shook his head. "I'm sorry Aggie. It was the damnedest thing. I had just passed the Boothe place when the thing snapped in two. It will take a week to fix."

Just passed Boothe House? A coincidence?

"Oh dear," Aggie sighed. "Every year we have a goblin or something for the little ones. It's filled with candy. Each one takes a swing at it with a stick until it breaks. All the candy spills to the ground and the young'uns scramble to pick it up."

"A piñata?" I remembered one from my childhood. My father had brought it back from his travels. I had a stomachache for a week after eating all that candy.

"It comes all the way from Spain. Last year we had a witch and wouldn't you know, it was the spittin' image of Duff." She laughed. "When I saw that crooked grin of his hanging up there

I wanted to take a switch to it myself."

"Are you spreading rumors about me again, woman?" Duff asked good-naturedly from behind the bar. It seemed he had heard that one before.

"I wouldn't dream of it." She rolled her eyes and winked at me. "Oh," she sighed. "I had to special order it too. I hate to disappoint the little ones. Duff? You have to take me to town!"

He looked at her as if she had asked to be crowned queen. "Aggie, you know I can't do that. We'd never be back in time. Besides, I have the fire in back to look after."

"You mean you're just too lazy," she scolded. He waved her away. "Maybe I should have taken a stick to him," she mumbled.

"I could take you," I offered. "We can be there and back faster than any wagon."

"I couldn't ask you to do that. I'm sure you have other things to do."

Like return to Boothe House and face Eric? I hadn't geared up my courage enough for that yet. "I don't mind, really. Lucille is almost out of petrol so I should go anyway."

She grabbed her coat and met me outside. "You want me to ride in that thing?"

"Of course," I replied. "She's perfectly safe."

She gave me a look that said she had her doubts.

"Come on, Aggie," I coaxed. "Where's your sense of adventure?"

"Hrmph!" She eased herself into Lucille and clung to the door handle for dear life. "Now don't go too fast."

"I wouldn't dream of it." The wheels spun and kicked dirt until they took hold and sped down the lane.

Once Aggie braved to uncover her eyes she actually enjoyed the brisk pace. I filled her in on the city news, when she let me get a word in, that is. After we picked up the goblin we did some window-shopping. Aggie saw a lavender silk scarf in the milliner's shop she said she would sell her right arm for. When I suggested she indulge herself and buy it, she laughed and shook her head.

"What would I be doing with a fancy scarf like that?"

"Wearing it for one," I said. "Why not Aggie? It would look wonderful on you."

"And it is such a lovely thing, isn't it?" I could see the wheels of indecision churning inside her head. "No, I better not. Next, I'd start getting airs and wanting a fancy coat and shoes."

Hers had seen better days, but I didn't say anything. "I see a telephone over there. I think I'll ring my father to see if he received my letter. Will you be all right?"

"Yes, you go on. I'll just have a look down here at the apothecary."

When I heard the chipper voice of our housekeeper I felt suddenly homesick.

"Is that you, Meredith?" she asked.

"Yes Margaret, how are you? Is the Colonel there?"

"Oh, he's upstairs packing. His train leaves in an hour. He should be there by supper time."

"Be where?"

"Why Hemlock. He said you were in some kind of trouble. What's going on up there, Meredith?"

"Nothing! I'm not in any trouble."

"Well your father seems to think so. There was some barrister asking all kinds of questions about you, where you schooled, what type of food you ate, books you read, music ... Your father didn't take to kindly to it when he heard."

"Eric!"

"Pardon me?"

"Oh nothing, Margaret. Get my father please?"

It was a few minutes before the baritone of authority reached my ears. "I'm on my way."

"Father, no! It's not necessary. I'm fine, really. My book is coming along splendidly."

"Who's this Boothe fellow? Is he giving you trouble?"

"No. At least nothing I can't handle. You know how suspicious those barristers are. I'm sure he was just making sure his house guest was not some criminal."

It took some doing but I managed to persuade my father to stay home. There was one condition of course, that I write every day. I agreed. Anything would be preferable to the Colonel storming into Boothe House. I could well imagine his confrontation with Eric. Two strong-minded bulls locking horns in a battle of wills. No, I had to avoid that at all costs.

The revelation Eric was behind all the little surprises was a boost to my ego. There was the piano, the dinner, the book. It hadn't been Graham at all. I should have been angry about his probe into my privacy, but I wasn't. I was elated.

I found myself in a generous mood. While Aggie shopped down the street I went to the milliner and asked him to wrap the scarf. Aggie deserved it, and the color really did suit her. I gave it to her on the way home.

"But you really shouldn't have," she protested.

"I wanted to."

"But the extravagance—."

"Is something we all need every once in awhile. Now I've had an exceptionally wonderful day, and I won't have you spoiling it with an argument."

She laughed. "Then you'll not get one from me. Thank you love. I'll treasure it always."

"I hope you'll wear it too."

"Oh, that I will. Now what is it that makes today so special? I'm sure spending the day with an old crow like me isn't the cause of those smiles I've been seein'."

"Aggie, you underrate yourself. I love your company."

"That may be so, but there's something else, isn't there?" She eyed me quizzically. "You hear from a boy back home?"

"Mmm, something like that, but he's not from back home."

"You mean you fancy someone here in Hemlock?" She clapped her hands with glee. "But, you've only just arrived. When did you meet him?"

"It was hard not to since we live in the same house," I said.

Her anxious smile fell to a frown. "Oh no, I should have known."

"What is it, Aggie?"

"I hope you know what you're about. Nothing but misfortune has befallen the mistresses of Boothe House."

"But I have no intention of becoming mistress. Why, I hardly know the man."

"And you'd be better off to stay that way. Alicia Mae learned that lesson the hard way."

"Alicia Mae?" It was my turn to frown. "The girl who committed suicide?"

"The one who was murdered," she corrected.

"You said it was suicide."

"Suicide, murder same difference. She's dead isn't she?"

Lucille's wheels locked to a halt just outside of Croakers. "But what does she have to do with it?"

"Ah love, didn't I tell you?" Aggie looked at me with eyes so sad, I felt a sudden lurch in my heart. "Alicia Mae was to be the next mistress of Boothe House."

❧ FOURTEEN ❧

The sun crouched low behind the spires of Boothe House reflecting subtle hues off the approaching clouds. It painted a picture of tranquility—appearances were not always as they seemed.

I returned alone in stunned silence, wanting to believe it was all a mistake. The sight of Eric brought all manner of questions to the surface. Why hadn't he told me of Alicia Mae? What was he trying to hide?

Watching him with the foreman, Mr. Harkins, unleashed a deep-seated fear in me, a fear that had planted itself the moment I stepped foot in Boothe House, but one I had refused to acknowledge—until now.

Their words were harsh and accusing. The argument escalated in tone to a point where I feared for Mr. Harkin's safety. An hour before I would have dismissed such notions, but now I was not so sure. Graham had spoken of Eric's temper. From how well I knew Eric, I couldn't conceive him of being a cold-blooded killer.

But exactly how well do I know him?

If measured by the amount of time we had spent together, it wasn't very well at all. Yet, I was aware of his honesty, his intelligence, and of course, his passion. He possessed a tenderness and deep emotion he revealed only to those close to him—things he revealed to me. Could that passion have led him to commit such a crime?

I didn't like the direction my thoughts were turning. If he had anything to do with Alicia's death it was purely accidental. Maybe it was something that just happened, something he hadn't meant to happen. No, Eric was meticulous about everything he did. All his actions were calculated in advance.

His own words came back to haunt me: "The perfect crime is one that looks as if no crime was committed at all." Like a murder made to look like a suicide? Was he truly a monster like his father before him?

The knife that had dangled before me since Aggie's announcement plunged deep into my heart. I slipped into the house and up the stairs. It was essential that I find Graham, and quickly. I cornered the housekeeper as she topped the stairs. "Ana, have you seen Mr. Ferguson?"

"Not since he left," she said.

My blood lurched into a panic. "Left? Where did he go?"

"There was an accident. One of the workmen was injured. Mr. Ferguson took him to hospital."

"Was it serious?"

She nodded. "His leg, I think."

"Oh, posh! What am I to do now?"

"I beg your pardon?" Ana gasped.

I had no time for her recriminations. Without offering an explanation I brushed passed her and ran to the sanctity of my room where I slammed the door and secured the lock. Leaning against it, I panted heavily. "Graham, where are you when I need you? You promised you'd always be here!"

The next mistress of Boothe House was found dead by the lake. The next mistress of Boothe House ...

The words kept echoing in my ears gaining in pitch until I could bear it no more. "Stop, stop!" I cried.

How could I have been so blind? I had allowed myself to be swept into a fictional romance, something I swore I would never do. My instincts had been duped into believing Eric as the flawless hero. God, what a fool I was! "Oh Madelaine, is that why you came back? To warn me?"

I felt rather than heard the knock on my door. The vibration shot through my shoulders down to my feet. I clutched my hand to my heart to muffle its rapid beating, shielding the sound that would betray my presence.

"Meredith?"

It was Eric! What was I to do? I stood back, not making a sound, listening and praying for his retreating footsteps. The knob creaked. I watched in horror as it turned one way, then the next, then stopped. I sighed. Thank heaven I had locked it!

"Meredith?" He knocked again only louder. "Are you all right? Answer me!"

With trembling hands I changed into my costume for the festival. The door was locked. I was safe. Eric would eventually tire and leave. I would then make my escape.

The festival was the perfect place to lose myself. Aggie would put me up for the night; then on the morrow I would leave Hemlock and all its misery behind me. Yes, that's what I would do.

"Meredith, I know you're in there. If you don't answer me I'm going to break down this door!"

I fumbled with my sash. Just a few more minutes and he would leave, I assured myself.

Wood splintered then gave way. He stood, breathing heavily, the remnants of my bedroom door at his feet. "Are you all right?"

Struck mute with shock, I could only nod in response.

"Would you care to explain all this? Why didn't you answer me?"

I opened my mouth but no words came out. After what I had learned, I thought I would feel differently about him, but seeing him standing there, his handsome face marred only with concern, changed nothing. I still wanted his arms around me, his lips against mine. The feeling was more frightening than the look of anger welling up inside of him.

He stepped closer holding out his hand as if to touch me.

Instinctively, I backed away. "You're not all right," he said, "You're as white as a sheet! I thought something was wrong when I saw you tearing up the drive."

I took a deep breath. "There's nothing wrong."

He captured my hands. "Don't tell me there's nothing wrong. You're trembling."

I pulled away as if the heat from his hands had singed my flesh. "Don't touch me!"

"Meredith, what is it?"

I turned so he would not see the tears welling up in my eyes. "I've just come to my senses is all."

"Your senses? Your senses about what? Meredith, what's happened to you? Last night you—"

"Last night was a mistake!" I swiped at my eyes with the back of my hand. "I don't know what came over me. It never should have happened and it never will again. Don't touch me!" I cried out as he reached for me again.

"Dammit, Meredith! Am I that horrible? Am I so wrong for the part?" Derision seeped into his voice. "I know I'm not some knight in shining armor from one of your books, but at least I'm human; that should count for something."

It counted too much.

The look of pain on his face wrenched my heart. I wanted nothing more than to throw my arms around him and soothe the hurt I caused. But I couldn't allow myself to fall under the Boothe spell again. I had to remember what had started it all in the first place. I had to remember Alicia Mae. "I have to go." If I stayed any longer, I knew I would lose what little resolve I had left. "I'll send for my things tomorrow."

I raced from the house before he could stop me. He didn't follow.

Torches lit the nighttime sky to a hazy amber. The festival had begun. There was laughter and music and people dancing to a lively folk song. I tried to get into the spirit of things, but my heart wasn't in the mood for gaiety.

The villagers were cordial, some even friendly, but with their subtle hints I was reminded I was not one of them. They were a secretive bunch, Aggie and Sarah the exceptions. How could I explain to these people that I knew more about Hemlock than many of them? Madelaine had taught me a great deal. I would always be grateful to her. If only I had one last look at her journal, I wouldn't have to leave with this shadow of mystery plaguing my mind, but there was no going back now.

Lavender silk bobbed through the crowd. I wove through to see Aggie kicking her heels in a dance. She threw me a wink. I would miss Aggie, too.

The droplets were few and far between, but it was evident the expected rain was near at hand. I was sampling a few sweets from the table as I waited for Aggie to finish her dance when I saw a familiar patch of flannel out of the corner of my eye. He wore the shirt, trousers and suspenders I had picked out for him. The mask and hat were even in place. Graham came! I was never happier to see anyone in my life. In my excited relief, I raced toward him.

His gait was more staid then I remembered. His hands were coiled into fists as if he were about to enter into battle, and the lips that were usually turned up in a laughing smile were set in a grim line. The greeting of relief fell from my tongue.

It wasn't Graham.

I darted into the throng of dancers to escape him. The music picked up and the step quickened. Each time I tried to pass I was swept into the crowd and passed from partner to partner. I searched for the familiar hat, but all I saw were the faces of the villagers who stomped their feet and clapped their hands to the music. The bonfire leaped high into the air. I could feel its heat and began to perspire. My steps faltered. A hand seized my wrist in a vise-like grip and jerked me up and spun me around. "Ouch! You're hurting me," I protested to my new partner.

When I looked up and recognized those furious grey eyes, I pulled to flee.

"Dance with me," Eric commanded. He tossed his hat over the heads of the crowd and placed a hand on my hip.

"I've had enough dancing for one night. Please let go of me."

"No. Not until you dance with me." He pulled me forward into the dance keeping pace with the music each step of the way. "Smile. Your friends may think something is wrong."

"What makes you think there isn't?" I asked, hating him for putting me on display like this.

His arm reached further around the small of my back and pulled me closer until our hips touched. I could feel the pounding of his heart through the light fabric of his shirt. He tilted his head down until we were nose to nose and stared at me with unforgiving eyes. "I'm through playing cat and mouse, Meredith. You never should have run away like that. Don't ever do that again."

"You make it sound like a threat."

He expelled an angry sigh and jerked his head up. Without a word he dragged me clear of the crowd toward the woods. He stopped at the base of a large gnarled oak and pressed my back against the trunk, bracketing my shoulders with his hands. Rain began a steady patter on the leaves. "You are going to tell me what all this is about or so help me God—"

"Or what? You'll beat it out of me?"

He backed away letting his hands fall to his hips. "Beat you?" he asked, his eyes crimped in disbelief. "Is that what you think? My God, Meredith! What crime have I committed that would make you think …"

"I don't know, Eric. You tell me what happened to Alicia Mae Pruitt."

"Alicia Mae? What do you know about Alicia Mae?" His eyes narrowed again but with suspicion this time.

I swallowed as he took a tentative step toward me. "Today I learned of your involvement with her. I know she was found in the lake and the villagers think she was murdered."

"And you think I did it? You're willing to believe idle gossip over my word? Christ!" He spun on his heels and dragged a hand through his hair.

I didn't know what to think anymore. It was hard to believe a man who could kiss with so much tenderness and passion could be capable of murder; yet, there was so little I knew about him. "Then tell me, Eric. Did you kill Alicia Mae?"

Rain began to pummel the earth. I was shielded from the elements by the mighty oak but not from the pain mirrored in his eyes. He threw his head up, closed his lids and took a deep breath. On a sigh he looked down into my eyes and said, "Yes, I killed her."

❧ FIFTEEN ❧

A denial, was the next thing I expected from his lips, but what came instead shocked me into dumb silence. "Call it murder if you like, but I'm just as responsible for her death as if I had held her under the water myself."

"Then you didn't actually …?

"Kill her? No, not in the physical sense. Sorry to disappoint you," he replied with biting sarcasm.

"I'm not disappointed, Eric. I didn't mean to imply that I wanted you to be a … a …"

"Murderer? You can say it, Meredith. Murderer. You were quite ready to sentence me without a trial a moment ago. Why can't you say it now?"

"Maybe because I never really believed it. How did it happen? Please don't turn away, Eric." I reached out to him as he started to walk away. The anger and mistrust I read in his eyes made me recoil.

He stormed back, rested a hand against the tree above my head and leaned down until we were face to face. "Why shouldn't I just walk away, Meredith? Why do you want me, a murderer, to stay?"

"But you're not a murderer!"

"Then why do you want me to stay? Tell me!"

Why did I want him to stay? Because I didn't want to be alone? Because I was afraid? Because I wanted him to want me again? "Because I … I—"

"You don't know, do you, Meredith? When you've figured

out exactly what you want from me I'll tell you everything that happened the last night I saw Alicia Mae alive. Until then, I give you my word, I won't bother you again."

"Eric wait!"

He stepped off through the woods into the clearing where the rain had turned into a full torrent. The last of the crowd was packing their gear up before heading home.

I picked my way past the puddles and wagons to Lucille. I climbed into the seat, slammed the door and sobbed. "Well, Meredith, you've really messed things up this time. There really is no hope for you."

I drove the distance back to Boothe House alone. Yes, I returned there, if only to release my own demons. My garden room was my sanctuary, the one place I felt safe and secure. Even that was threatened, I thought, as I looked down at the shambles of my bedroom door.

With a dry night gown on I climbed into bed, shivering more from sadness than the cold. The sound of a door closing signaled Eric's return. I waited with baited breath, wondering if he would suddenly appear at my door. His footsteps sounded down the hall followed by the closing of another door. He wasn't coming. I sighed with relief. Or was it regret?

What was I to do? "Oh, Madelaine, please help me," I beseeched. "Help me to understand." Slowly, as if my prayers were being answered a haze of sweet ginger filled the room. I closed my eyes and let the dream mist claim me.

Music and laughter grew louder and louder as I merged into Madelaine's world. My feet began to move in step. They were dancing, he and Madelaine. I could feel her anxiety, her fear and her excitement when their lips first touched. Guilt tore at her conscience, but she knew everything would be all right because she was with him. And being with him seemed so right. A love like this could never be wrong, she said over and over again.

The rain fell in sheets drenching them both. The hunter's lodge appeared out of nowhere as if it was meant to be. Their clothes dried by the fire as they lay in each other's arms. It was a contented place to be, there beside the man she loved. She felt safe and free from all the misery at Boothe House. This was where she belonged.

Then I saw Eric's face. They way he laughed when I covered him with ashes or pushed him into the water; the way he looked at me just before a kiss and the way he held me after. And then I saw the way his eyes clouded with hurt when I accused him of a crime he surely could not have committed. Was it love that made me want to go to him and confess my sins? Was that where I belonged?

I bolted upright in my bed. The sheets were in a tangled heap on the floor. The hair around my face was damp with perspiration.

With a match shaking in my hand, I lit the bedside lamp and turned the flame all the way up. My legs felt uncertain beneath me. I went to the bathroom to splash cold water on my face. It did nothing to soothe the war raging through my mind.

With pen in hand I went to work on my book, describing the scene of Madelaine and her lover, putting to words what was only now becoming clear in my heart.

Sun warmed my hand. I lifted my head off the page and blinked at the early morning rays. I had fallen asleep at the desk. With a yawn, I rose and stretched. I padded to the bathroom and stepped on a splinter. "Ouch!" I noticed it then, the door on the floor amongst splinters and broken pieces of molding. It was a reminder of the night before and what an utter fool I had been.

I didn't really believe Eric had been responsible for Alicia Mae's death, but I had yet to hear the whole story from his lips.

My instincts told me something was still very wrong about the whole mess, but I hadn't a clue as to which direction to turn.

When I came down to breakfast, Eric was already seated at the table. I turned to go back upstairs.

"You may come in, Meredith. I was just leaving."

Blast! The man had the eyes of a hawk. "I wasn't leaving because of you," I explained.

"Of course not. Just like I'm not leaving because of you," he supplied. He folded his napkin and placed it on the table next to his plate. His food had barely been eaten. "You look tired, Meredith." The concern in his voice made my heart weep a little more.

"I didn't sleep much last night," I replied.

"It must be an epidemic."

I looked up to see fatigue lines creasing the corners of his eyes.

"Is there something else you prefer?"

"Hmm?" I asked.

"Your plate. You were eyeing it with trepidation. Did Linnea sneak something into your eggs again."

"Oh. No ... How did you know?"

"She's not very good at hiding her jealousy."

"Jealousy of what?" I didn't have a lifestyle many women envied. "She's afraid you'll take Graham away. He's been like the son she never had. Graham is quite smitten with you if you haven't noticed. I guess we all were."

Were? Was I now part of the past tense of his life? "Graham and I are just friends, nothing more."

"Nothing?" he asked.

"Nothing," I assured him. "Eric, I'm very sorry about last night."

He shrugged as if all that transpired between us didn't matter, but I could see the wall of indifference he erected to shield himself. "So am I, Meredith. So am I"

A summons at the front door called Eric away. When he

returned he held several telegrams in his hand. "It looks as though we won't be the only ones at the party. We've just received our first responses and all of them are coming."

"Are any of them interested in buying the house?"

"No. These are just colleagues of mine."

"I guess this means we are indeed going to have a party," I remarked.

"You're staying then?" he asked.

"Only if you want me to."

"You know I do."

"Then I'll stay."

Eric shifted on his feet. "Good."

"Will we be ready in time?"

"We should be if Harkins heeds my threats to finish the work."

"Is that what you were discussing with him yesterday?"

"Yes, a man was injured."

"I know. Ana told me. What happened?"

"Pure carelessness happened, that's what. A scaffold slipped and the man fell. It was an accident, nothing more, but according to Harkins, the scaffold was deliberately tipped by a ghost."

I swallowed hard. "A ghost?"

He nodded. "Unless you think I had something to do with it?"

Lord, how the man hated me. "That was unfair."

He nodded. "You're right. I apologize. I'm just tired of being falsely accused. Now rumors are being scuttled through the workmen about the house being haunted. It seems the closer we get the more obstacles we run into. Harkins refuses to return."

"And if he doesn't?" I pondered to ask.

"He will." Eric looked so sure of himself. "I don't think he'll risk being sued over a few superstitious rumors."

I wished I held his confidence.

We heard the first scream just as the clock chimed nine. Shackles rose up my spine.

"What the devil was that!" Eric exclaimed.

The second scream sent us scrambling to the second floor. It was a woman's scream, a terrified choking sound coming from the master bedroom. All I could think of was the day I had been locked in that room, feeling those icy fingers close around my throat.

We reached Ana who was hovering over one of the new maids in the hall. "What happened?" Eric demanded.

Jennie, the maid, sobbed while Ana shook her head. "I don't know my lord. The girl swears someone attacked her in the master bedroom but when I went in, there was no one there but herself."

The poor creature's eyes were still wide with fear. She clutched her throat as if protecting it from further harm.

"What kind of rumors has she heard?" Eric asked.

"I wouldn't be knowing about that," Ana replied. "I don't listen to gossip."

Jennie finally found her voice. "It wasn't a rumor," she half choked. "That evil thing tried to kill me!"

"Oh, for Christ sake!" Eric said hotly. "Has everyone gone mad? Meredith, explain to her that there is no such things as ghosts."

How could I when there was such overwhelming proof before my eyes? "Well ..."

"Not you, too!"

I tried to reason with him. "When I first came here you even said—"

"So there is a ghost!" Jennie cried.

"No, there isn't!" Eric bellowed. "I was just trying to ... Never mind what I said. I'm telling you now that this house isn't and never has been haunted. If you are too weak-kneed to overlook some silly superstitious nonsense, Miss Tilly, you are free to find employment elsewhere."

"That suits me just fine," sniffed the young maid.

My heart went out to the girl as she departed down the hall

with slumped shoulders of dejection. "Did you have to be so harsh?"

"What would you have me do? Pat her on the head for a job well done? She'd have the entire staff in an uproar with her foolish ranting. I won't abide such insolence."

"Eric Boothe, you may be angry with me, but it's no reason to take it out on a young impressionable girl."

"I am not angry with you, Meredith!"

"Then why are you shouting?"

"I'm not …" He lowered his voice when several of the staff appeared to see what all the commotion was about. "I'm not shouting. I just can't believe you would give credence to that girl's blathering."

"It wasn't just blathering. She was telling the truth. Where … where are we going?" I asked as Eric gripped my arm and pulled me down the hall.

"To my father's room."

I tugged at his hand for release. "I don't want to go there!" I would have been perfectly happy to never step foot in that room again.

"I'm going to prove to you that the image of haunting spirits rests solely in your mind." He thrust me into the room.

Nothing had changed. Everything was freshly cleaned and in its proper place. Daylight poured through the spotless glass. Nothing looked unusual.

"You see," he said. "No ghosts, no evil spirits. You have a vivid imagination, Meredith. You just let it get the better of you."

"Then how do you explain the bump on my head?"

"Bump? Where?" he asked with concern. His hand brushed over the no longer noticeable injury. "I don't feel anything."

"It's gone now but I tell you it was there. I was locked in this room and when I tried to get out I felt something cold around my throat. When I passed out I hit my head on the floor. You can ask Graham."

"I intend to."

That wasn't the first time he questioned my integrity.

"I didn't mean to insinuate I didn't believe you," he assured me. "I only meant that I should have been informed. I'm surprised Graham entertained the notion of ghostly spirits."

"I didn't tell him the ghost caused me to faint," I confessed.

Eric gave a great sigh. "Maybe because it didn't? Come here." He took my hand and led me to the fireplace. The portrait of Edmund Boothe loomed overhead seeming to scrutinize our every move. It must be difficult for Eric to even consider the fact that his very own father has come back from the dead.

"Put your hand down here near the opening," he instructed. "There, do you feel that?"

A cool draft of air rushed down the chimney across my palm.

"The damper has been stuck open for as long as I can remember. What you felt was a rush of cold air coming down the chimney. When there's a good wind outside the force is enough to ruffle the bed linens."

He gave a good argument. It seemed plausible, but I was not convinced. "Then how do you explain the loud cackling I heard?"

"I would suspect a bird or small animal made that sound from the chimney. I wouldn't be surprised if there was a nest of some sort up there now."

"But—"

"Meredith, did you actually see a ghost?"

"Well, no—" *Not here.*

"See any objects fly across the room? Lamps light themselves? Hear any distinctive voices?"

If I had, would I dare admit it now? I shook my head. "Do you have to be so logical about all this? Not everything in this world can be explained so easily."

"I haven't encountered anything that couldn't."

Perhaps I had let my imagination take advantage of me after all. I would have continued to believe that if I hadn't heard the same words I had spoken just moments before, but now in

Edmund's voice, a harsh whisper discernible to my ears alone. *"Not everything in this world can be explained so easily."*

There was no use in trying to explain about the gooseflesh on my arms. In a voice that cracked with apprehension I explained it was, "just a chill." Eric would need physical proof besides my trembling hands. Of course I hadn't any to prove of what I heard. He wouldn't believe me if I said I recognized his father's voice. Nor would he believe me if I told him how his mother visited my dreams and even showed herself in the mirror. But all of it was proof enough for me to believe the spirits of his parents lived on at Boothe House. Edmund's intentions still weren't clear, but I sensed they boded ill. Especially for Madelaine.

By afternoon the news of Jennie's departure had spread through the skeletal staff. They continued their duties with a constant eye over their shoulders waiting for some spectral presence to overcome them too. They spoke in hushed whispers and moved like skittish colts from room to room. Not one dared to voice suspicions for fear of reprisals from the lord of the manor.

Eric tried to ignore the discontent in the house, but when the new kitchen maid dropped a stack of dishes after hearing a harmless creak of floorboards, he became furious. Mounting tension twitched in the side of his cheek. His usual self-control was fading quickly. I felt partly responsible. My own nervous behavior only spread more suspicions through the house.

It was best to keep my distance from him. I only seemed to bring out the worst in him. I took a brisk walk around the grounds wading through beds of fallen leaves, some wet and sticking to my boots from the rain the night before. What a shame, I thought, as I stepped over thistles and creepers where once a beautiful garden grew. There was little hope for it now.

There was still the greenhouse, though that had yet to see a workman's hand. I couldn't find a clean spot on the windows to see through. Paint had been used to shield the inside from view. Whoever had used it last certainly wanted privacy. The door was still locked, just as I had expected. It was just as well. If I had seen what poor condition it was truly in, I may have been moved to rolling up my sleeves and setting it to right. There was enough work waiting for me in my room. Books do not write themselves, though this one nearly did, thanks to Madelaine.

I started back around to the front of the house when I got the distinct impression I was being followed. A quick glance around assured me I was indeed alone. I moved on listening to the crunch of my footsteps, thinking I was just being silly when I heard a crunch that was not my own. Stopping again, I looked around, peering through the vacant trees for some foreign shape lurking about. The experience I'd had when first arriving at Boothe House seemed to repeat itself. Someone or something was tracking me.

My eyes darted from tree to tree catching a glimpse of movement. Was someone there? No. It was just the play of leaves falling to the ground. With each gust they fell like a torrent in a hundred droplets of sound. Perhaps that was all it was. Yes, perhaps.

Back in my room I worked on my manuscript until I had no more to write. Madelaine's story was left in limbo as was I. She had found love again and had to give it up. But did she? I wondered. I had left the journal at a crucial point and I was ever eager to get back to it. This was the perfect opportunity with Graham still away. His lengthy absence puzzled me. I hoped he hadn't befallen any misfortune. Eric mentioned Graham might stay on a day or two while in town, for whatever reason, Eric didn't know. Could it have something to do with his "surprise," I wondered.

As I took the well-tread path to Graham's room, I averted my eyes from the master bedroom door and the goings on behind it. I vowed, as did many of the staff members, never to set foot past that threshold again.

Once inside Graham's room I took a seat on the bed as usual and opened the drawer, anxious to begin where I had left off.

The journal was not there. My hand searched the entire space of the drawer and found nothing. The journal was gone.

I began to panic. "Calm down," I scolded myself. He must have just moved it. It was not under the bed or on his shelves. In desperation I rummaged through the drawers of his bureau, pushing aside scraps of paper and trinkets, piles of neatly laundered handkerchiefs and unabashedly rifling through his undergarments. It was gone! Blast!

"Hello, Meredith." His voice was low and held little of its usual humor.

My heart sank to the floor. Culmination of guilt came to rest on my shoulders. I looked up at Graham hoping some reasonable explanation would miraculously occur to me for why I was there.

In his hand rested Madelaine's red velvet journal. "Looking for this?"

❧ SIXTEEN ❧

The look on Graham's face struck fear in my heart. Since the first time I met him I had never been afraid of his intentions or whatever harm he may be capable of. But there was an anger in him now that frightened me, and not just an anger towards me. He battled some inner demons.

"You're home." I tried to be pleasant and casual as if I hadn't just been caught with my hand in the cookie jar, so to speak, but I was afraid guilt was written all over my face. "I worried that something might have happened to you."

"Did you?" Sarcasm spewed from his lips. It wasn't like Graham at all. "And here I thought you'd welcome the chance to spy through my drawers." He stepped into the room just far enough to close the door; the journal still clutched in his hand.

I unconsciously moved back. "I'm sorry—"

"You can relax, Meredith." He walked to the bedside table to pour himself a brandy from the decanter. My eyes followed the journal. "I've known for some time that you've been sneaking in here to read this."

"I feel so ashamed. I—"

"Well, don't. It's only human to be curious. I applaud your tenacity. I didn't know you had it in you." He broke into a grin before tension reclaimed his features.

"Why did you try to make me believe the journal never existed?" I asked.

"I didn't want to let the skeletons out of the closet before I

162

was good and ready. You've read it. I'm sure you can understand my reasons. But that didn't stop you did it, you little imp?" A trace of his old humor returned.

I hadn't had the chance to read all of it, but now my curiosity was even more piqued. "How did you find out?" I wondered. It must have been Ana, the little snitch.

"How is irrelevant. In fact, it's all irrelevant. You may as well take the book. It's of no use to me now."

He dumped the journal into my arms. He would never know what a precious gift he gave me. I cradled the journal in my arms as if it was made of fine porcelain. "Thank you."

Graham shrugged. "I had hoped it would be a means to keep Boothe House, but I've been advised the evidence is not sufficient to ... well, never mind. Eric may have won another battle, but he has yet to win the war. I shall have to think of something else, is all."

"Living in a new place may not be so bad. You might enjoy the change of scenery," I said.

His face clouded over. "You know nothing about it, Meredith," he snapped.

Nor did I want to. As far as I was concerned the house was nothing but a catalyst for misery. Eric was right to want to sell the place. "I'm sorry. I didn't mean to interfere."

"No, I'm sorry," Graham apologized. He ran a hand through his tousled blonde hair. Weary lines were beginning to show on his face. "I shouldn't have spoken to you like that. Meredith, would you mind ... I don't believe I'm saying this. I finally have you in my bedroom and what do I do but ask you to leave so I may get some sleep. I'm afraid my accommodations were somewhat lacking last night. There's nothing like sleeping in your own bed, you know. Can you ever forgive me? I promise to make it up to you."

At least his flirting powers were still intact. "Oh, I think I can manage." I offered some thoughts of encouragement, too, upon parting.

Graham was resourceful and may succeed in keeping Boothe House. Deep down I hoped he would fail, for his sake if not for Eric's. It was rather devious of me especially after he gave me the journal.

The journal. I finally had it all to myself. A new sturdy door had replaced the broken one to my room and I steeled behind it to settle in the corner chair of my garden room with my feet curled up beside me, intending not to move until I had read the last page. Flipping over page after page, I tried to find the place where I had left off. Madelaine had just discovered something. I was on the verge of exploding with curiosity.

> *November 4*
> *The ball was wonderful. And so was Edmund.*

No. I already read that.

> *September 1*
> *Edmund has informed me we will again host a masquerade.*

No, no that wasn't it either! That happened just before the festival when she met him. Oh, where was that page?

> *December 20*
> *I have suspected for some time ...*

Yes, yes, that was it!

> *.... but now I am most certain I am with child. Sarah has confirmed the same conclusion. I'm overjoyed. This child is truly special and comes at a time when I most need someone to love. My stomach rebels morning, noon and night, but I don't mind. It is the seed that grows inside me I am most*

grateful for. Edmund shall surely find favor with me now.

December 21
Edmund was not only pleased, he granted me my own room. He has even given me permission to redecorate as I choose. I think I will select the room at the other end of the hall, the one farthest from the master bedroom. It's the largest of the guestrooms that overlook the garden. I know just how I will decorate it too. Something floral and green, for green is a symbol of hope.

December 25
Christmas day. We had a very nice supper. Edmund was pleasant and in high spirits. The prospect of a coming heir seems to agree with him. He talked on and on about his coming son.

If he only knew.

I would be just as happy with a daughter, a little girl to spoil and pamper, but Edmund will not accept anything less than a son. He says he must produce a son to win his father's approval. I find that odd since Ignacious Boothe has been dead for over three years.

February 10
Edmund has insisted once again I take a dose of his special brandy, as did his mother and grandmother and great grandmother when they were with child. It was Boothe tradition. I humor him by pretending to drink it; then I spit it out when he isn't looking. I refuse to endanger the life of my

child with that vial brew. It made me deathly ill
once. There's no telling what harm it could do to
the baby.

March 27

I felt the baby move! At first, I thought it was
just my imagination, but when I placed my hand on
my stomach I felt a little kick. Sarah laughed at my
look of amazement. "Isn't it wonderful?" she asked.
How right she is. To think that a life is growing and
moving within me outshines everything I thought
was important before. Being able to share the
experience at the same time with Sarah makes it
even more meaningful.

April 17

Edmund has been traveling less. I take refuge in
my bedroom from his constant harping. He never
bothers me there. It's the one place I can call my
own. The gold clock is now on the mantel where I
can see it no matter where I sit. I try not to dwell on
what "might have been". I have the child to think
about now.

May 9

Edmund has chosen the name Frederick. I didn't
bother to tell him I have already chosen the name
of Eric, and if it should be a girl, Iris, but I am most
certain it will be a boy. Motherly instinct I suppose.
Edmund says his father has approved of his choice.
I am beginning to worry. This is not the first time he
has talked about his father as if he were still alive.

June 2

Sarah has another son! Sean is what they have

named him. I almost missed it. My movements are
rather slow and awkward these days, a sign my
time is coming soon. I wish Sarah could be by my
side when the time comes, but Edmund has already
hired a doctor and no other to tend me.

July 14
What started out as a twinge in the early morning
turned out to be a long grueling day of endless pain.
There was even a brief argument between Edmund
and me over the name. I was a bit heavy handed in
my dealing with the situation. Not knowing anything
about childbirth, Edmund believed me when I said
I would not birth the baby unless he would let me
name the child Eric. It was a promise I had made
the moment I knew I was expecting. Edmund of
course agreed and at two-twenty in the afternoon
Eric Edmund Boothe entered the world.

I cry each time I hold him in my arms. I have been
truly blessed. He is so small and precious. From the
dark patch of hair to his light grey eyes, he is the
image of his father. I will love and protect him for
the rest of my life, and for that reason Edmund must
never know the truth.

I turned the page. There was nothing more. That was all she
wrote. But the story didn't end there. She left one vital clue. After
she spent the night with her lover, I had suspected as much. And
there were other subtle hints here and there to strengthen my
suspicions. But when I read of Eric being the image of his father
with dark hair and light eyes I knew I had been right. Edmund
was light of hair with dark eyes.

He wasn't Eric's father.

Graham must have deduced the same conclusion and that
was why he needed the journal to hold on to Boothe House. If

he could prove Eric was not the rightful heir, he stood a good chance of claiming Boothe House as his own. And according to Graham that was a fortune. But he also said the journal was of no use to him anymore. Perhaps the evidence was not substantial enough. The facts were sketchy at best. Madelaine never directly denied Eric's parentage, nor did she name her lover. Graham had no way of tracking down concrete proof.

But I did. I had Sarah. If I could find out who the man was, I may be able to solve the mystery of her disappearance. I owed it to Madelaine. She had brought me this far. I was determined to go the distance. Her son would learn the truth about his mother and father.

I had to see Sarah at once. Slowing only long enough to put on a coat and grab my bag, I raced down the stairs to the door.

"Meredith, where are you going?" Eric stopped me as I reached for the door.

"I have to go out for awhile."

"But it's dark out. Can't it wait until tomorrow?"

"No, it really can't."

"I don't suppose you want to tell my why?" he asked.

"No. I don't." Not just yet anyway.

I was relieved to find Sarah at home and alone.

"Have you had your supper yet?" she asked.

"No, I haven't," I replied. "But I didn't come here to eat."

"I could put another chop on. It would be no trouble," she offered. I accepted, knowing she would probably refuse to eat herself if I did not join her. We engaged in the usual small talk as she prepared the meal. She seemed pleased to be able to cook for someone beside herself.

"Sarah, the reason I came was to talk about Madelaine."

"I already told you all I can. I don't know anything more."

"I think you do."

She turned away from me with downcast eyes. "I don't know

what you mean—"

"Please believe me, Sarah," I begged. "I mean Madelaine no harm. I know there was another man in her life. They loved each other deeply. I think that's wonderful. If anyone deserved a moment of happiness, it was Madelaine."

"You've been listening to rumors again," she said.

"It was no rumor, Sarah. I also know that Eric is not Edmund's son."

Her composure began to deteriorate. "Who told you that?"

"Madelaine did."

"Madelaine? Then she's come back?"

I hated to squash the hope in her eye. "No she hasn't come back. I don't think she ever will. It's very hard to explain. I wouldn't blame you if you didn't believe a word of what I'm about to tell you. Sometimes I find it hard to believe myself. Madelaine didn't tell me in the flesh but in spirit." Disbelief shifted to her eyes. How to explain it?

"You see it's all been revealed to me in a dream. Ever since I came to Boothe House my dreams have been filled with Madelaine and her life. I believe she wants me to find out the truth of what happened for Eric's sake. He's very bitter over her disappearance. He believes she ran off with her lover and purposely left him behind. And you and I both know the truth."

I hadn't gotten through to her yet.

"You expect me to believe Madelaine came to you, a complete stranger, instead of me, the one person who knew and loved her all these years?"

Good point. One I couldn't answer.

"If Madelaine came to you as you say then you should know everything that happened. Why are you asking me?"

Another good point. "I don't know. Maybe she's afraid to for some reason."

The kettle in the kitchen began to spout a high pitched whistle. "Excuse me," she said as she went to turn down the fire.

"Can I help?" I offered.

"No. The tea will be ready in a moment. I just have to turn the chops. You just sit."

But I couldn't. I was too agitated to sit down. I paced the floor trying to think of a way to gain Sarah's confidence. She didn't believe me; that was obvious. What else could I say to convince her? I found myself back at square one.

My eyes roamed the gallery of pictures on the wall. If Ian were still alive, maybe I could convince him, I thought. I came to the picture of Sarah and the handsome gentleman. "You know," I said to Sarah, "Madelaine didn't even finish her journal. The last entry was Eric's birth." The gentleman in the picture seemed vaguely familiar. "Sarah, who is this?"

She came to the doorway. "You have Madelaine's journal?" Her voice quivered.

"Mm, hmm." There was something about the man's eyes. "She showed me where to find it. It was in the bottom of her trunk in a secret compartment of all places."

"That journal was like a Bible to her. She kept its hiding place secret." Her voice was just above a whisper.

The black and white photograph was hard to distinguish but his eyes looked light in color, blue or even grey.

I instantly knew where I had seen them before. "The man in the picture, who is he?"

The pallor drained from her cheeks. "That's my brother Eric—Eric Jeffries

✷ SEVENTEEN ✷

"It's him, isn't it? He's Eric's father," I said.

Sarah began to sob. I went to comfort her. "It's all right, Sarah."

"I swore never to breathe a word of it," she sputtered. "I promised."

"Sarah what happened? Did they run away together?"

She dabbed at her eyes with her apron and sat her small frame heavily on a chair. "I don't know."

"Please, Sarah, it's very important."

She shook her head. "I honestly don't know. Eric came back to the house after meeting Madelaine. He said he was taking her and the boy away. They were going to start all over again as a family. Some place far away where Edmund couldn't find them. That's the last I saw of him."

"They never contacted you?"

"No. About a week later a rumor surfaced about Madelaine running off. The boy was still at the house. Then I knew something must have gone wrong. Neither Madelaine nor Eric would leave their son behind."

"So Eric knew about his son?"

"Oh yes, Madelaine told him when he came back to Hemlock."

"Tell me about him. What was he like."

Sarah now relaxed; obviously talking of her dear sibling was a joyful task. "He was full of mischief as a young lad. Always had a smile, especially for the girls. My mother spoiled him.

Eric knew just how to charm her into anything. He was like that with most of the women he met, including me. There wasn't anything I wouldn't do for him. He had a way of taking on any challenge head on and usually won, too."

Like father like son, I mused.

"Tough as nails when the going got rough but sweet as a lamb with those he loved, especially with Madelaine. Oh, he was taken with her right off. I should have seen it coming. Kindred spirits, they were. I should never have invited him to visit. Then maybe ..." Her voice faded off with regret.

"You mustn't think that way, Sarah. I believe things happen for a reason. Like finding the journal. There's a reason Madelaine wanted me to find it. She swore at the end to love and protect him for the rest of her life. I think it has something to do with that. You can't blame yourself for them falling in love. I know Madelaine never regretted it. Eric gave her a son."

"I never thought of it that way. Living all these years praying and wondering about them, never knowing what happened ..."

"What did happen? Why didn't Madelaine leave with him the first time?"

"She was a married woman. She took a vow to stay with Edmund until death. Eric wouldn't give up, though. He swore he'd come back for her. He had a job that took him away to New York to build one of those new skyscrapers. He was an architect, a very good one. It would take two years, but he couldn't pass up the small fortune they offered him, the fortune for him and Madelaine.

"He wrote to me nearly every week. He put letters in for Madelaine too, but she refused to read them. She never really believed he would come back for her. But I knew he would. Eric never went back on a promise. When the baby was on the way she made me promise not to mention a word of it to Eric. I didn't, even though I thought he should know. No, Madelaine was going to raise the baby as a Boothe. He would have a title and position. She was thankful for that.

"The war came then and Eric went off to fight. When his duty was through he came straight to Hemlock for Madelaine. It had been nearly eight years since they'd seen each other. Can you imagine that? Eight long years and you would have thought it was only eight hours after seeing them together. Their love never died. It only grew stronger."

It was becoming clearer now. "So that was when they ran away together?"

"They waited about a week until young Eric came home from school. But for some reason, they left without him."

"Did Edmund try to find her?"

"Not that I know of. He never once came to ask if I knew anything, not that I would have told him if he had."

The pieces were falling into place except for one. Where did they go? They couldn't have just vanished into thin air. There had to be a clue. Maybe it was in the journal and I just didn't see it. I would read it again and again if I had to. I must find the answer, I silently vowed. For Eric.

I stayed to accept Sarah's hospitality to supper. When it was time to leave I promised Sarah I would return with what I hoped would be a happy ending.

The temperature had dropped. Ice-like rain began to fall. I shivered as I ran to Lucille and started on my way back to Boothe House. Something still nagged at me. Edmund hadn't tried to find Madelaine. That piece didn't fit.

How would Eric take the news? To find out the father he knew and loved was not his real father would be a devastating blow. I would have to choose my timing carefully and only after I had all the pieces together, for how could I tell a man he wasn't the titled lord he thought he was.

What came next happened so quickly I knew not how they occurred. The turn came too fast, or maybe the sleet on the road had turned to ice. When I tried to slow down Lucille I swerved to the left off the drive. I found myself driving through throngs of brush and low lying branches, picking up momentum as I headed down the incline. My door became dislodged from the jarring terrain and flew open. In my feeble attempt to close it, I steered Lucille into the path of a large gnarled oak. There was no time to react. Closing my eyes, I waited for the impact.

It was sudden and loud with the sound of crunching metal. My body was hurtled forward then out the open door. The back of my head made contact with the butt of the door handle.

Heaven was very cold and damp. Or maybe it wasn't heaven at all but another place for wretched souls.

"Meredith."

Someone here knows me! "Hmm?"

"Meredith, open your eyes."

It was Eric. *Dear God, is he dead too?*

"Meredith, wake up!"

I strained against the forces that pulled me back. My eyes fluttered until focused. I was in my garden room safe and sound. My body still trembled. "What happened? I thought I was dead."

"Another hour laying out in the cold and you would have been," Eric replied sharply.

What was he so angry about? "Sorry to disappoint you."

"Drink this." He set a glass of amber liquid in my hand.

"What is it?"

"Brandy."

I wrinkled my nose. "I don't want any."

"Drink it!" he ordered. "It will warm you up."

I was in no position to disobey. The liquid had a bitter, ugly taste. I sputtered as it burned a trail down my throat. "I liked the sherry better."

"This is stronger. Drink a little more."

"More?" I braced myself for another assault; but surprisingly, it wasn't as bad. It started in my toes, a rising fire that traveled up my legs through to my fingertips leaving me with a warm cozy feeling. I took another swill then another. The brandy seemed to improve with each taste. *Maybe just one more.*

Eric grabbed the glass from my hand. "That's enough." He set the glass on the table and corked the bottle.

"You're not going to take that away are you?" *Perish the thought.* And just when I was getting used to its unusual taste. "Why don't you join me in a glass?"

"No, thanks. I never drink it and I think you've had enough for awhile."

"Oh. Well, you don't have to yell at me."

"I was hardly yelling."

"You look very angry to me."

"That's because you gave me quite a scare." He scowled. "It's a good thing Graham found you when he did."

"You mean you were worried about me?" I liked that idea. Eric didn't seem to think my amusement funny, however.

"Don't feel too pleased with yourself. What you did was foolish. I told you not to go out," he reprimanded.

"Yes, Eric, you were right as usual. Aren't you tired of being right all the time? It's rather tiresome from my point of view." I leaned back and stretched upon the bed feeling the last of the thaw. My skin, now warmed to a high degree, tingled from the smooth flow of silk over my body. Silk? I chanced a look under the blanket to see if maybe I was mistaken. I wasn't. "Eric, where are my clothes?"

"They were soaked. I had to remove them."

God, he was handsome! Even when he was frowning. "Pity I had to miss that," I replied, feeling giddy from the effects of the brandy.

Eric cocked one eyebrow. "Feeling better are we?"

"I don't know about you, but I'm feeling better, thank you." Yes, I was feeling much better indeed. The back of my head was still tender, but none the worse for wear. That brandy had remarkable medicinal powers. "Come to think of it, I am still a wee bit cold."

When I reached for the glass Eric pulled it away. "You've

had enough, too much if you ask me."

"I wasn't ... asking you that is. I've hardly had any at all. I feel fine, better than fine!"

Now he was smiling. "Oh, I don't doubt that. But wait 'till tomorrow."

My tongue showed him what for. "Killjoy!"

Eric's laughter turned into a cough as Graham entered with a tray. "See Eric," Graham said, "I told you she would be all right."

Eric was quick to disagree. "She's not out of the woods yet."

"She will be with me taking care of her." Graham smiled. "So feel free to go back to your business. I'll stay here with her now."

Eric leaned against the wall in a defiant move with arms crossed against his chest. "I think I'll stay a little longer if you don't mind."

Graham frowned. "Suit yourself. But you know, two is company, three's a—"

"Graham, did you bring that food for yourself or do you plan to share it?" I interrupted, tired of their bickering.

Graham looked down at the tray then back at me sheepishly. "Sorry. Here you go." He placed the tray on my lap and proceeded to help himself to a biscuit. "Would you like me to feed you?"

"No, I think I can manage," I said, glancing in Eric's direction. He had retreated into the shadows with only his lower half visible in the light. He still retained the casual but guarded stance. "I heard I have you to thank for my rescue," I said to Graham. I tried to jog my memory of being rescued. All I could remember was the rendering crash of metal. *Lucille!* "How bad was it?"

"Not too bad from what I could see. It could have been worse. We won't know until tomorrow. Eric will have a truck come and pull her out."

I made a silent prayer for Lucille's welfare. I would never

forgive myself if something happened to her.

The bouillon was delicious. It would have been better with biscuits, but all of them managed to find their way into Graham's mouth.

Suddenly, I was feeling very strange. Maybe the brandy was beginning to wear off. My head began to throb and my muscles ached. I wasn't feeling so very wonderful anymore.

"What is it, Meredith?" Graham asked, seeing my change of expressions.

"I guess the accident took more out of me than I thought." Though his face was hidden in darkness I could just see Eric's smug smile and nod of "I told you so."

"Is it your head?" asked Graham as he proceeded to check for injury.

I brushed his hand aside. "No. I'm just tired. I think I'd like to sleep now." My stomach began to rumble.

"Of course," Graham said, settling himself down for the night in the chair. "You go ahead. If you need anything I'll be right here at your disposal."

With increasing cramps shuddering through my delicate system, company was the last thing I had in mind. "Well, actually—"

Eric seemed to read my mind. *Bless him.* "Why don't we leave the lady to her privacy, Graham. I'm sure she would appreciate some time alone."

"Very well. If that's what you want," he directed to me.

"If you don't mind."

The second the door closed behind them, the first wave hit. I cleared the bed in one leap and dashed to the bathroom just as my stomach rebelled. And then just when I thought there was nothing left to expel another wave hit, and then another, until finally, I lay trembling in a heap on the floor. My arms and legs felt heavy and ached with searing pain. My stomach and bowels cramped up with fatigue. Was I going to die after all?

When I was sure the attack had subsided, I crawled on my

hands and knees back to the bedeoom. It was cold, so very cold. I changed into the warmest nightdress I had and slid under the covers of the bed, pulling the heavy woolen blanket close about me.

What was happening to me? It couldn't have been the accident. I was barely bruised and my head did not hurt or feel fuzzy like the last time. No, it must have been something I ate. All I had recently was the brandy and bouillon, an odd combination to be sure, but hardly cause for such a violent reaction.

The how and why was not important. Tomorrow would be soon enough to examine my own foolishness. If I survived the night, that is. The prospects for that looked rather bleak at the moment.

It was well past midnight when I was awakened by the feel of something cool against my forehead. It felt so nice and reassuring against the backlash of pain and fear I was suffering. I looked up and gave Eric a weak smile. "How long have you been here?"

"A little while. I'm sorry. I didn't mean to wake you," he said, removing a cloth from my forehead and placing it in a basin by the bed. "Go back to sleep."

"I'd rather not, if you don't mind. I'm afraid I won't wake up."

"Feeling that bad, are you?"

"Worse."

"Well, your fever is down so I think you're through the worst of it. I'll be right down the hall if you need anything."

"Wait!" I straightened up in bed and reached for his arm. "You're not leaving, are you?"

"I think under the circumstances, I should," he replied. His hair was tousled; his day clothes wrinkled and his eyes were tired and red.

"Please stay," I begged. I couldn't bare being alone. "Just for a few more minutes? We could just talk or something. Please?"

"Very well." He rubbed at his eyes and sat in the chair by the bed. "What is it you want to talk about?"

I rolled onto my side to face him. "Tell me about Alicia Mae. I promise to believe you this time."

He chuckled a bitter angry laugh. "You're asking too much of yourself, Meredith. You may convince yourself to believe, but you still don't completely trust me. I can see it, there in your eyes."

"Then help me to. Tell me about Alicia."

"There isn't much to tell. I came home about three weeks before the wedding. One night Alicia came here and said if I couldn't give her what she asked, she would kill herself. I didn't think she was serious. If I had, maybe I could have prevented it."

"What did she ask for?"

"Boothe House, me and the life of a rich lady. I couldn't give it to her. So, I'm the one responsible for her suicide. They found her the next day. There was an inquest. Linnea verified that Alicia left of her own accord and neither Graham nor I left the house after her. Graham recovered from the shock easily enough so I went back to the city and didn't return until just recently. End of story."

"Is that all?"

"That's all I'm willing to say on the matter. The episode is dead and buried and I prefer to leave it that way."

"Was Alicia ever in this room?" I queried, wondering if perhaps she, too, had been privy to Madelaine's presence.

"Not to my knowledge."

"This was your mother's room, wasn't it."

He studied me long and hard. "Yes."

"Do you miss her?"

I noticed his jaw tense and his hands open and close into fists. "I'd rather not talk about my mother."

"I miss mine," I said. "It happened rather suddenly. One day she was feeling a bit under the weather, and the next she was gone. I was only ten at the time."

"I'm sorry."

"I guess having her gone makes me appreciate the time we had together more. Of course, I'd give anything to have her back again. Would you?"

He gave a long, great sigh. "The truth is ... my mother thought more of lying and cheating than she did of me. When I was about seven she ran off with a man she barely knew. And unlike you, I wouldn't give a shilling to have her back."

"Don't you ever wonder what happened to her?"

"No, I don't. As far as I'm concerned she died the day she left. Both she and Alicia are part of a past not worthy of remembering. I'm very satisfied with the way my life has turned out. I have no desire to spoil it."

He was still bitter, and my desire to see him healed almost made me tell him the truth about his father. His contented life could very well change, though, and not to his liking. Then again, perhaps he already knew the truth about his parentage and my probe into the secret only drove the bitterness to the surface. "Do you still hate me?"

Eric rubbed at his eyes then leaned over on his elbows. "I don't hate you, Meredith." He said it with such gentle conviction I started to believe it. His fingertips touched my forehead. "Your fever is gone. Now, go back to sleep."

"But—"

"Shh. Close your eyes."

My eyelids drifted closed and I fell into a deep but troubled sleep thinking of how I had hurt Eric and how I was going to make it up to him.

The illness had all but disappeared the next morning. Tired aching muscles and a weary stomach were all the remembrances left of the wicked after effects. I eyed the bottle of brandy and the empty bowl of bouillon with malice. Never again would either of those two pass my lips.

I thought about Eric and his bedside confession. He had been stung by two women in his life. No wonder he felt so easily betrayed. And now I was going to turn his world upside down again by exposing the truth about his mother and father. Would he thank me? Or shun me?

I wanted so desperately to get our relationship back to where it was before. Where exactly that was, I wasn't sure. Sharing secrets and laughter with him was a remarkable experience that I didn't want to part with. His kisses, too, transported me into another dimension of my life where I yearned for afternoon walks, children at play and tender whispers in the night. And I wanted it all right now, this second, before the chance for love escaped me or betrayed me. Something inside Boothe House refused to let happiness grow, and I was its next victim.

I made my way to the bath for a long hot soak. My progress was slow. No sooner had I finished the long arduous task of climbing into the tub when Graham knocked on the bathroom door. To my dismay, he was quite insistent. "Can't it wait?" I asked.

"I thought you might like to know we pulled Lucille up to the house." His voice was a bit muffled through the solid wooden door, but I understood enough of it to delay my bath.

"Is she all right?" I emerged from the bathroom tying my robe.

"There's some extensive grill work that needs to be done, but I think she'll make it."

"Oh, good."

"There's something else," he added. "I think you better sit down." The urgency in his voice gave me cause for alarm. "When I was looking over Lucille for damage I noticed something."

"What?"

"Someone had cut one of your brake cables. Now, I'm not an expert, but I believe that's what caused you to lose control."

"Who would do such a thing?" I wondered. "Are you sure it wasn't just broken?"

"No it was deliberately cut. Do you know of anyone who might want to hurt you?"

"No. Why would anyone want to hurt me?"

"I don't know. I was hoping you could tell me. Do you know or have something that may make someone angry?"

"N ... no."

"Well, I've given it some thought and although it pains me to even consider it, it's the only reasonable explanation. Think about it, Meredith, the journal. You and I both know what's in there. There's only one person I can think of who may want that information buried for good."

"No! That's impossible."

"Meredith, it has to be. He's the only logical choice."

"I won't believe it. It can't be Eric!"

❧ EIGHTEEN ❧

"For your own safety, Meredith, believe it," Graham said. "He must be worried about what you know. Do you know something I don't?"

"N ... no," I lied.

"Are you sure? Maybe there's something in the journal I missed."

It wasn't in the journal. Sarah was honor bound to keep the secret. I refused to break her trust. "No. I know nothing more than you do. So you see, Eric has no reason to want to hurt me."

"I know you feel indebted to him for letting you stay on here—"

"That isn't it," I said. He didn't know of Eric's and my involvement. If he did he would see how ludicrous his accusations were. He would also be very hurt. "We've become ... friends. I can't believe he would do something like that."

"Desperate men do desperate things," Graham replied. "You have no need to fear him. I'll protect you."

"I don't think that will be necessary," I assured him.

"For your sake, I hope you're right."

Graham visited often to check on my improvement. Each time he came he tried to convince me of Eric's involvement in my accident. I tried to find fault with his reasoning, but he drummed on and on until I too began to have doubts.

Eric's sudden coldness towards me did little to ease my fears. I saw very little of him. When I did we were never alone. Graham was always close at hand so there was no chance for a private word. And if it weren't for my own initiative I wouldn't have seen him at all. The workmen had returned just as Eric predicted, so I assumed the magnitude of work yet to be done kept him away. Or was it a guilty conscience?

Then there was my illness. How strange it was I should fall so violently ill after drinking the brandy Eric had given me. Could it have been the work of Edmund's private stock? If I recalled correctly, Madelaine too had suffered from the brew. I eyed the bottle suspiciously. It did have an unusual flavor.

I poured a sample into an empty perfume bottle and placed it in my purse to be tested. The ingredients were sure to be medicinal herbs meant to heal, not harm. Eric would not have given it to me otherwise. Would he?

It was a ridiculous notion. Graham's nagging suspicions were getting the better of me. It was still worth having it tested, even if just to discover its uniqueness. I didn't really believe he intended me any harm with it. It was just a set of coincidences. Eric would have a very logical, intelligent explanation for it all. If I saw him long enough to ask, that is.

As I walked the halls marveling at the changes taking place, I also became aware of other changes unseen by the naked eye. Where Boothe House was once cold and unwelcoming, it was now filled with the blistering heat of intolerance. With every new change I could feel the anger rise, heaving and pounding like a spoiled child who refused to give in. And I was not alone. Many a questioning glance passed from servant to servant when unexplained "accidents" occurred. In fear of losing employment, not a word was spoken, but heads nodded in agreement that these were just a prelude of things to come.

I hibernated in my room, in my sanctuary. That, too, seemed threatened by the turmoil growing outside my door. Grief and fear were constant haunts. As I held Madelaine's journal in my hands I couldn't help but wonder how close I was to discovering the truth. The answer had to be here somewhere. But where to find it? I paced and fretted trying to discover that one important clue, but to no avail. I needed Eric's keen mind. I needed his powers of deduction, his rational thinking. If only I could go to him. If only ...

Restless days turned into restless nights. I found myself sleeping less and fretting more. The illness had weakened me, body and soul, but I dared not close my eyes for fear of what awaited me. The truth lay in the dark only I was too afraid to travel the distance. And each time I closed my eyes the nightmare returned. The smell was sickly sweet, the vision hauntingly fresh.

The voice was small and slight but the plea for help was loud and clear. Her empty cup returned to the table with a clatter. "Eric?" But how could that be? Madelaine looked at the mantle clock. He was not due home for another hour. The anguished cry called out again. "Eric!" she cried as she ran from her room guided by a dark premonition.

His room was empty. There were no more sorrowful cries, no pleas for help. Had she imagined it all? A flash of grey, uniform grey, passed the door. "Eric, wait!" Madelaine called to him. He would not answer. She moved to follow, slowing only to listen for the sound of his footsteps. They came light and faint, ascending to the third floor. Her heart quickened to meet each step. When she reached the top stair she grabbed hold of the banister as a bout of dizziness engulfed her. She breathed deeply until it passed. This was not a time to fall ill. They were within hours of being free of this house and Edmund's dominance. Nothing would keep them from their freedom.

The door to the ballroom was open. Her footsteps echoed through the empty room. Each call to her son was answered with silence. She followed the sound of a creaking pulley into the kitchens. The dumb waiter had been lowered. Eric and Graham had often used it in their games. She had no time for games now. It was not like Eric to trick her this way. "Eric! I want you to come up here this minute! Eric?" It was no use. He was down in the cellars and out of earshot. She would have to go down and fetch him for he was obviously not of a mind to come up himself.

As Madelaine descended through the house she was oddly aware of the quiet. Not a sound or body stirred. It was unusual for this time of day. A second wave began to build. Her head began to swim and spasms shuddered through her. She had to find Eric and quickly. She would feel better once they were away. She was sure of it.

Madelaine opened the heavy door to the cellar and peered down the darkened passage. Step by cautious step she descended the stairs. The flicker of a candle led her deeper into the catacombs that channeled under the house. She didn't like being down here. This part of the house was foreign to her. She turned to see her last footsteps disappear into blackness. Her footsteps tried to keep pace but the candlelight always seemed just ahead of her. At last, it came to rest in a small room. She entered with a shaky hand on her stomach and a reprimand on her lips. Before she could voice a word the door slammed shut. The force of the blow extinguished the flame, the only light she had left. She whirled about and scrambled for the latch only to hear the lock turn with a final click. "Eric, open the door!"

she ordered. "Eric!" Her pleas fell on deaf ears.

The scrape and thud of an object against the door startled her. "Eric, what are you doing?" Another scrape and thud followed, then another. What game was he playing now? More sounds followed, one after another. "I insist that you open this door immediately! Eric?"

"I'm sorry Madelaine, but that won't be possible."

Madelaine began to tremble. "Edmund? Edmund, please let me out!"

"What? And leave your lover in there all by himself?"

Lover? She stumbled in the darkness, dropped to her knees and crawled across the floor searching.

"I'm going to grant you your wish, Madelaine." Edmund's voice was oddly calm. "You wanted to spend the rest of your life with him and so you shall."

Her fingers made contact with a body. Cold and lifeless. With a sob she cradled her lover's head in her lap. "No! Please God, no!" She rocked back and forth.

The scrapes and thuds became loud, Edmund's voice more distant. "It was very foolish of you Madelaine, to think you could ever leave me. Did you honestly believe I would allow you to take my son away?"

Panic moved her into a frenzy. "Eric! Edmund, what have you done to him?"

"I've done nothing to him but everything for him. Soon you will be just a vague and bitter memory to him."

He was insane. She had to reason with him somehow, but she couldn't think. Another wave

*struck, this time gripping her chest. "Edmund
please!"*

*"Good-bye Madelaine," were the last words she
heard before the final brick scraped and thudded
into place.*

Unable to bear it anymore, I came out of the nightmare
panting in terror and filled with a nauseating sickness. For
so long I had wondered what happened to Madelaine, Now I
knew. I did not have to search any longer for the place to which
Madelaine and her lover fled, for they had never left Hemlock.
Their last agonizing hours were spent here in Boothe House.

Tears came in a great rush. How she must have suffered! It
sickened me to think about it. The most disturbing of all was
that Edmund had not acted alone. He had enforced his evil on
another. Someone had lured Madelaine to the cellar—a child.
There were only two children at that time, Eric and Graham. It
pained me to think that either of them could be capable of such
a heinous act. The man I loved or the man I called friend; which
one was it?

It was well past midnight when I looked at the mantel clock.
Everyone should have been fast asleep, yet I heard a voice,
small and slight—a child's. Was I still dreaming?

It came again, a small cry for help. The voice lured me to the
door. I turned the latch, but the door wouldn't open. The scent
of ginger was very strong almost pungent.

Do not go!

"Madelaine?" I called out. I looked toward the mirror, toward
the bed. Her spirit was here in the room. I could not see it but
I could feel it, heavy and shielding, pulling me away from the
door.

The child called again, more insistent, almost challenging
me to find him. With determination I overpowered Madelaine's
will and flung the door open. I had to know who it was. With a
lamp in hand guiding the way, I stepped from my room into the

darkness of the night. The voice led me down the length of the hall. "Eric? Graham?"

My feet moved of their own accord to follow the swiftly fleeting cry. They came to a stop at the far end of the hall in front of the door that was once Edmund's bedroom. The master bedroom. I hesitated.

The cry came again from inside the room. I pressed my hand against the door. My need to know was stronger than my fear. Edmund was dead and it was just a cry from the past. There was nothing to fear.

I turned the latch and opened the door. The room was still, deathly still and empty. Slowly and quietly, I moved. The cries stopped. "Eric? Graham?" The whistle of wind blew passed my ear.

I jumped at the feel of something brushing against my cheek. The window had been left open. I let out an exhausted breath and commended myself for not bellowing a scream. That's all it had been, a November gale whistling through an opened window. It seemed odd I should hear it at the other end of the house. I felt a movement advancing quickly from behind. Turning, I caught the towering form of my attacker, arms poised in midair clutching a long steely weapon—Eric.

This time I did scream.

The curtains billowed. "Wait!" cried Graham as he leapt out of the shadows.

"Graham!" thundered Eric as he lowered the poker to his side. "What the bloody hell are you doing here? Meredith, are you all right?"

He reached out to me, but I jerked away. I couldn't take my eyes off the sharp point of the poker resting on the wood floor. It had been so close. To think that he had just been about to ...

"Meredith, I'm sorry," Eric said. "I didn't mean to frighten you." His eyes softened as he approached, but I had not forgotten how, just moments before, they were filled with murderous intent. I backed away.

"Frighten her?" Graham placed a protective arm around my shoulders. "My God man, you nearly killed her. Or was that your intent?"

"Don't be absurd," spat Eric. "I saw movement behind the curtain. If anyone was nearly killed it was you, hiding behind there like that. And you still didn't answer my question. What are you doing in here?"

"I thought I heard something, a noise, a voice or something."

I turned to look up. "You heard it too?"

Eric eyed us critically. "There were no voices. It was the wind you heard."

"Don't listen to him, Meredith," Graham pleaded. "He probably made those sounds just to lure you in here. Lucky for you I heard them too."

Eric's hand tightened around the brass handle of the poker. "Yes, that was a stroke of luck, wasn't it?"

"You see," Graham exclaimed, "he admits it!"

"I admit nothing!" The poker skidded across the room from Eric's wrath. "This is ridiculous. Meredith," he said grasping my shoulders. "I would never hurt you. You know that don't you?"

"I don't know anything anymore."

"Meredith, please!"

Graham brushed Eric's hands aside. "Don't you think you've caused her enough grief this evening? Come, Meredith, I'll take you back to your room."

I murmured a brief "thank you." As we moved to pass, Eric clamped a hand on Graham's shoulder. "I'm watching you," he warned.

"Is that a threat, cousin?"

"Take it as you wish."

By now several members of the staff had gathered at the door voicing their concerns over the most recent scream— mine. Graham pushed me through, leaving Eric to answer their questions.

Once inside my room Graham closed the door behind us. "Now do you believe me?"

I dropped into the corner chair and buried my face in my hands. "Oh, I'm so confused."

"Don't fret over it, Meredith. The important thing is that you believe it now."

"Do I have a choice?"

"Not that I can see." Graham could not hold back his joy over the situation. He smiled and rubbed his hands together with relish. "I've got him now."

"Forgive me if I don't share your enthusiasm."

Graham dropped to his knees before me. "Yes, of course. I'm sorry. How inconsiderate of me, especially after all you've been through. I guess the prospect of Eric finally getting his dues is making me a little anxious. If only I had that final piece. Meredith, are you sure you know nothing more?"

"Yes, I'm sure."

Why was I protecting him? Perhaps it was because I still loved him. A small part of me wanted to believe Eric was innocent.

Graham cupped my hands in his. They were cold. "You do trust me, don't you?"

Could I trust anyone anymore? "Y ... yes, but ..."

"Then think Meredith, think! There must be something."

"Well, there is one thing—"

"Go on."

The door hurled open. Eric.

Graham straightened to his full height. "There is such a thing as knocking you know."

Eric's eyes scanned the room to see if anything was amiss; then they came to rest on me. "I thought you might be in danger."

"From me?" Graham asked appalled. "We've already established the fact that it's you she's in danger from."

"Just what sort of lies have you been spreading?" Eric growled.

"No lies. Just the God's truth."

"I'm warning you Graham. I'm on to your little game and I won't stand for it."

"More threats, cousin? You're failing in your attempts to plead your case. Meredith doesn't stand a chance of believing you now."

Eric looked at me, his eyes beseeching me to understand. "Meredith, you must listen to me. You are in danger, but it's not from me."

Graham laughed. "She's no fool, Eric. She knows who the real villain is here."

"Stay out of it!" Eric hissed. "Meredith, please! You've got to believe me."

God, how I wanted to believe him! "I'm trying to." I caught sight of Graham's self-satisfied grin. It disturbed me to see his enjoyment of another's pain. "I just can't think right now. Please leave, both of you."

And they did. I was alone once again in the twilight of the night, wrestling with my thoughts on how fragile trust can be.

I awoke late the next morning not remembering having fallen asleep. It was a restful sleep, for I had already determined my next course of action. I was leaving Hemlock. Boothe House fought the battle and won. It poisoned Eric's mind against me as it had against Madelaine. And the only way I knew how to save him was to leave.

Without sparing a moment, I went to the armoire and removed my suitcase. Opening it on the bed, I began to pack my things. I did not stop even when Graham knocked on the door.

"What are you doing?" he asked.

"Packing."

"But you can't leave. You're my only hope!"

"I can't stay!"

"Then ... then marry me."

"What?"

"I'm serious Meredith. You know how I feel about you. Together we can reclaim Boothe House. Think of it."

I didn't have to. My answer was no. Graham was nice—too nice. I liked to lose at checkers once in a awhile. I liked my praise to come from the heart and not just given to win my favor. I liked to be part of a team and not elevated to stand alone on a pedestal. I liked to be kissed in a way that set me apart from every other woman. Only one man was capable of all that, and it wasn't Graham. "It's very sweet of you, really, but I can't. I'm sorry. Too much has happened here. I think it would be best if I just go."

"No, please! If I can't persuade you to be my wife at least stay and help me reclaim Boothe House. You owe me that much."

And risk having my heart completely broken? "I can't."

"You've got to. Last night you were about to tell me something. Something about Eric. What was it?"

"It was nothing. Just a dream I had." A horrible nightmare.

"What sort of dream?"

"I dreamt of Madelaine's murder."

He blinked. "Her ... murder?"

"Yes. She never left Hemlock. Your uncle killed her before she had a chance to."

It took him a moment to digest the news. The shock quickly wore off. "Are you sure about this?"

"Yes, I'm sure. Look, if you don't believe me—"

"Yes, yes, I believe you. I just find it difficult to imagine my uncle killing anyone."

"Well he did. And the worst part of all is he didn't act alone. Someone lured her to him."

"Oh? And did you see this person?"

"No, only glimpses of a child. Madelaine believed it to be Eric." I ached inside each time I thought of it.

"Have you told anyone about this dream? Eric perhaps?"

"Heavens, no!"

"Good. We don't need to give him another reason to kill you. This changes things considerably."

"But he was just a child then ..."

"A child capable of sending his own mother to death. It pains me just as much as you, but we have to stick to the facts. First it was Madelaine and now you. He won't want that information to leak out."

"But I won't tell anyone."

"It doesn't matter. You know and that puts you in danger. Just like you know my uncle was not his real father. For that he was just in jeopardy of losing Boothe House. Now, the stakes are much higher. He can't afford to let you live."

Graham paced about the room in deep thought. "I must plan this very carefully. We don't want him to catch on to us. He's very clever, you know. He'll try to cover up his tracks. We mustn't let that happen. I'm afraid there's no avoiding it—you'll have to stay."

"No, no I can't!"

"You have no other choice. You'll have to carry on as though nothing has happened. At the ball tonight I want you to play the perfect hostess."

"Oh, please don't make me do that! I don't think I can."

"You can and you will. We can't have Eric become suspicious."

"And what will you do?"

He brushed my cheek with a gentle sweep of his hand. "The only thing left for me to do—reclaim Boothe House." He looked at me then with something akin to regret. "It's a pity you declined my offer of marriage. You would have made the perfect mistress for Boothe House. A fact I think we'll both regret."

The door stayed ajar as as he retreated down the hall. My only regret was in coming to Boothe House in the first place. But I didn't regret all of it.

As if reading my unspoken thoughts, Eric stepped into the doorway. I was unprepared for the assault of emotions his closeness evoked. I was angry. I was frightened. I wanted to be comforted—by him.

"You're leaving?" he asked, seeing the open suitcase.

I nodded. "My book is almost finished and the two months are nearly over anyway …"

"I was hoping you would at least stay for the ball."

"I am. But after what happened last night I think it's best if I leave first thing tomorrow."

"Meredith, you do believe that I would never intentionally hurt you."

I shook my head slowly, uncertain of what to believe. "I want to believe that, Eric. But I need time and distance, and I think you do, too."

He shrugged. "If only I could. I'm afraid what I need right now I'm about to lose."

"Excuse me, my lord," Ana cleared her throat. "But there's a gentleman at the door who says he has a message for you. I told him you were busy but he said it was urgent. From London I believe."

"London? Tell him I'll be right down." Eric turned to me. "Stay here. Promise me you won't leave this room."

I swallowed. "Why?"

"I don't have time to explain. Just do it."

"But—"

"Please Meredith."

I gave him my word. And then I left.

❧ NINETEEN ❧

I drove Graham's motorcar through Hemlock to the outskirts of the village, rehearsing the speech I prepared once more as I pulled into the Bradley farm. Sarah would be devastated to hear Eric and Madelaine's plans for the future had come to an untimely end. I would spare her the details, of course. She did not need to know how much they had suffered, but there was no easy way to speak of murder.

"Sarah?" I called through a crack in the door. There was no answer to my knock so I stepped in. "Sarah?" As I walked through the kitchen to the parlor I heard movement. "Sarah?" A man stepped out from around a corner. We bumped. "Oh, I'm sorry." I recognized him immediately. He was Sarah's son Jonathan.

"Can I help you?" he asked.

"I was looking for Sarah. Is she here?"

"No. No she isn't. I'm sorry, I didn't catch your name ..."

"Meredith. Meredith Barlow. And you must be Sarah's son Jonathan." I extended my hand in greeting.

"Yes. Were you a friend of my mother's?"

"Yes, I ... am. Is she here?"

He took a deep breath. "I'm afraid not." He looked tired and distraught. "Miss Barlow, my mother passed away a couple of days ago."

Passed away? Sarah dead? "But I just saw her a couple of days ago."

"It was a shock for us, too. She was buried yesterday. I'm sorry if you weren't notified. I tried to contact everyone my mother knew but ..."

"No, I'm sorry. Tell me, how did she ... how did it happen?"

"The doctor believes it was some sort of stroke. A woman from the village found her Thursday morning there in the hallway."

"I'm so sorry. Is there anything I can do," I asked.

"Thank you, no. Everything has already been taken care of."

Everything hadn't been taken care of. I didn't get the chance to tell Sarah about Madelaine and Eric. It was ironic; she died just hours after breaking a silence she had lived with for so many years.

Just when I thought I had no more tears to spare they began anew. Remorse and sorrow rained down my cheeks. I shouldn't have pressed her so. It must have been the stress. But she seemed quite well when I left her.

Sarah was gone. I was the only one left now who knew the name of Eric's real father—the one who held Eric's future in the palm of a hand. It was cause enough for a desperate man to resort to desperate measures.

The tears were unstoppable. I reached into my purse for a handkerchief and came across the vial of brandy I had put in there days ago. Edmund's elixir of life. What was in it that would cause Eric to give it to me and not take any himself? This could very well be the proof I needed.

It was over an hour's drive to town. Eric would surely notice I was gone and had taken Graham's car. This was my only chance. I had to know. I fled down the dirt road with great speed, kicking up stones and dust in my wake as I headed toward town.

I parked just outside the apothecary and went inside with my vial in hand. The white-haired gentleman bid me a good afternoon. "Can I help you Miss?"

"I hope so. I was wondering if you could tell me what is in this vial."

The man eyed the vial carefully and lifted it to his nose. "It appears to be brandy," he said.

"No, I want to know what's in the brandy."

"You mean you want me to analyze the contents?"

"Yes."

"I'm sorry, I can't do that."

"You are a chemist, aren't you?"

"Well, yes but—"

"Then you do know how to break down substances?"

"Yes, but what you're asking is highly irregular."

I threw myself on his mercy. "Please, it's very important. I wouldn't ask if it wasn't of the utmost urgency."

"I suppose I could take a look at it."

I sighed with relief. "Thank you."

"It may take me a couple of days—"

"No! You don't understand. I need to know right away."

He shook his head. "That's out of the question. It would take at least a couple of hours—"

"Fine!" I said before he changed his mind. "I'll be back in two hours."

I went to the corner shop for a bite to eat and to pass the time. Drumming my fingers on the table, I kept an eye peeled on the apothecary across the street. I glanced at the clock. I had four hours before the first guests were due to arrive at the ball. That didn't give me much time.

An hour passed. I moved the small cuts of ham around on my plate as a play of interest. My heart just wasn't in food at the moment; it was sitting impatiently across the street behind the closed door of the apothecary. Two hours was a very long time.

After my failed attempt to keep myself occupied, I went to the garage to check on Lucille. I hadn't seen her since my accident. I wasn't prepared for the shock. Her grill was a tangled mass of metal. The man working on her told me about the brake cable.

He confirmed Graham's suspicions. "That was a nasty prank someone played on you. If both cables were cut you could have been killed."

When I asked the man if a rock or something could have accidentally cut it, he said it was possible, but not likely.

"No, I would say it was deliberately cut," he stated.

That meant someone cut it. Eric? What more proof did I need? A witness. A good trial always needed a reliable witness. I hadn't actually seen him cut the cable, but I had seen him pour the glass of brandy. Oh, what was taking so long? I glanced at the apothecary. There was less than an hour to go. I walked around the town looking in the shop windows. I stopped in at a bookstore and the milliners where I had purchased Aggie's scarf. Nothing interested me but the apothecary two doors down.

It had been over two hours. The closed sign still hung on the door. I tried to tell myself to be patient, the waiting would be worth it. The evidence I needed would be in my hands. And if it was harmless? Then I could still hold on to that little sliver of hope. And if it wasn't? Then it would mean the final break of my heart.

After three hours the sign was finally removed. I hurried back to the apothecary, my breath held in anxiety every step of the way.

"This is a very interesting brandy you have here," the man remarked. "Where did you get it?"

"It was given to me."

"Then I suggest you dispose of it immediately. It has faint traces of conium maculatum in it. Ordinarily, I wouldn't have found it; but I noticed these specs of sediment here. It's not really sediment at all. I suppose you would probably be able to taste it, but I wasn't about to take the chance."

"What did you call it? Coni ... what?"

"Conium maculatum. Maybe you're more familiar with its common name—hemlock."

"Hemlock? Are you sure?"

"Oh, quite. I can't tell if it contains a lethal dose or not; one drop of coniine from hemlock can be fatal so I wouldn't recommend drinking any of it."

"No, of course not." Edmund had and he survived. Of course, he was also insane. No wonder Eric refused to drink any of it. "Thank you."

Well that was that. I had all the proof I needed now. Graham would be delighted with this extra bit of evidence. Something concrete to pin him to.

I should have despised Eric, but I didn't. I guess I would never really believe Eric's malevolence towards me was of his own doing until he drew the last breath from me himself. The vial was still in my hand. Perhaps he just had.

By the time I returned to Boothe House many of the guests had already arrived. One of the new maids met me in my room. She neared a state of hysterics.

"Thank heavens you're home, Miss. His lordship has been most upset by your absence. He had the whole staff looking for you."

"Has everyone arrived?" I asked.

"I think so. His lordship is just waiting on you and none too patiently, I might add. Shall I tell him you're here?"

"Yes, tell him I'll join him in the ballroom shortly." *To say good-bye*.

"Yes, Miss. Will you be needing help with your costume? I hope you don't mind that I took a peek. It's very lovely."

"Thank you. It was the last mistress's."

"Well I'll bet the current master won't be able to take his eyes off you all evening. I can help you on with it if you like?"

"No. I think I can manage. But there is one thing you can do for me." I went to the desk and scribbled a note to Aggie asking if she wouldn't mind my staying with them for the night. Staying in Boothe House another night was out of the question. I then handed it to the maid. "I want you to find someone to deliver this to Aggie Towns at Croakers in the village. Do you think you can do that?"

She nodded.

"And be sure not to show it to anyone. Do you understand? Not anyone."

"Yes Miss. I'll take care of it straight away."

While I ran my bath I pulled out my suitcase and finished the packing I had started earlier.As I went to put my manuscript in the suitcase, I paused; inside was a story of one woman's life, her tears, her joys, her sorrows. Madelaine's story would never be published. I would keep it as a remembrance of the wonderful story it could have been. Maybe I would even finish the last chapter. But there would be other stories. There always were.

When I came out of my bath I noticed a box on the bed that wasn't there before. It was long and narrow, tied with a pretty pink bow. The unexpected gift made me immediately suspicious. I examined it carefully before I dared to open the lid. Inside was a delicate glass slipper fit for a princess—someone like Cinderella. There was also a note:

> There's a very special surprise waiting for you. Meet me in the wine cellar tonight at midnight.

I crumbled the note and threw it back in the box. Surprise indeed! My hands began to tremble. Why, Eric? Why do you want to do this to me?

I changed into my costume and vowed to be long gone by midnight. With the tall wig finally secured to my head I looked in the mirror. The gown was breathtaking. Marie Antoinette, the woman who lost her head. *Lord, what made me think of that now!* I had to regain my composure. Eric was waiting for me upstairs.

A knock sounded on the door.

"Who is it?"

"It's me, Graham."

I let out a sigh of relief and unlocked the door.

"Marie Antoinette?" he asked. "How fitting."

"Please, Graham, I'm in no mood for your jokes. Why aren't you dressed yet?"

"I'm saving it for a surprise. I just came to make sure that you haven't backed out on me."

"The thought did cross my mind. Here, look at this." I handed him the note. "Eric left this in my room."

He read it out loud. "... you'll have to meet him."

"No!"

"You must! This may be the only way to catch him red-handed. Don't you see? The cellar is the perfect place to commit a murder."

Another knock came at the door. "Excuse me, Miss?" It was the maid again.

"Yes, what is it?"

"His lordship is getting most anxious for you."

Graham whispered, "Go. Don't let him get suspicious."

"All right," I replied through the door. "I'm coming."

Before I left, Graham rested a reassuring hand on my shoulder. "Remember, midnight. Don't be late." He smiled then added, "I'll be waiting for you."

I fixed the rhinestone mask over my eyes and headed for the ballroom. The orchestra was just beginning to warm up as I climbed the stairs. The ball was well under way. But I had a more disturbing thought to deal with: The cellar was the perfect place for a murder.

The room became enchantingly alive with brightly colored costumes and sounds of laughter. The chandelier, now restored to its former magnificence, glowed with a hundred candles. Ivy-covered trellises stood in each corner. Tables flowed with every kind of hors d'oeuvre imaginable. No expense had been spared.

Eric stood amongst a crowd of masked faces dressed to

perfection as a sea-going pirate. His dark hair was covered by a shimmering gold scarf but for a few waves along the back. A loose-fitting shirt opened to the middle of his chest; and close-fitting leggings, indecently close, hugged his long limbs. A patch covered one eye over a day's worth of stubble giving him the dangerous look of a worthy buccaneer. I could not miss noticing the long saber sheathed at his side, an instrument of death.

Laughter turned to anger when our eyes met. He fixed me with a lethal stare riveting me to my spot. In two strides he was at my side, glaring down with admonition. "Are you all right?"

"Yes, I'm fine."

"Where the devil were you? I had the whole house in an uproar looking for you."

"I went on some errands—"

"Was Graham with you?"

"No. I went alone."

He sighed. "You promised you'd stay in your room."

And he promised he would never hurt me. "You needn't have worried. I was quite safe."

"For now," he murmured. "Come here, there are some people I want you to meet. One of them is a Dr. Porter Hathaway. He was the last interested buyer. His presence here leads me to assume he's still interested in Boothe House."

Dr. Hathaway was a stout middle-aged man with a set of little round spectacles perched on his nose. He was dressed as a lamb with curly white fleece and black-spotted ears. He had a humorous disposition and, I thought, should he really be interested in Boothe House, he was going to need it.

I was also introduced to a number of colleagues from the legal set, businessmen with their wives and school-hood chums. There were so many of them it was hard keeping all their names straight. My attention was not on the task, of course. My preoccupation with the clock prevented me from retaining any one thought for longer than a minute.

At half past nine Eric signaled the orchestra to begin the

first dance. He took my hand and swept me into a lovers' waltz, holding me intimately close. His voice lowered to a seductive cadence. "We have some unfinished business between us."

The possibility of what could have been nipped at my reserve making me warm with memory and sad with regret. "Yes, we do." Our business was far from over. I agreed. I had to know why he was trying to kill me.

Dance after dance played. I was shuffled from one partner to another. One persistent wolf, Steven, was always under foot. To avoid him I sought out the docile lamb, Dr. Hathaway. He asked me a number of questions to which I eluded the answers. Yes, Boothe House was remarkable and yes, it had character. It had many characters.

"Can I ask you something doctor?"

"Yes, of course."

"Are you familiar with the poison, hemlock?"

"Somewhat. Why, are you planning to poison someone?" He chuckled.

"Not exactly. It's an idea I have for a new book. I was wondering how much you had to take before it would kill you."

"Well, I'm not exactly sure. Coniine is a very lethal poison. One drop is generally sufficient. But how much hemlock does it take to make one drop? I'm not sure. One bite, a leaf or two, I don't really know."

"What if someone were to drink it over a long period of time. Could he lose his sanity?"

"I would think that he had little sanity to begin with if he drank it voluntarily."

"But is it possible?"

"I suppose it's possible but not likely. Hemlock strikes the muscles. It paralyzes them until death. The mind is rarely affected. It could last for hours. Some vomiting and blindness does occur, but in most cases, if treatment is begun in time the patient usually survives."

"And what if he doesn't drink enough to kill him?"

"Then he's in for a very uncomfortable and painful ordeal."

That much I knew from experience. So the brandy was not the cause of Edmund's insanity. He had come by it naturally or through what Graham called the "Boothe curse." And where did he get it? Hemlock had been gone from these parts for decades.

A light tap on my shoulder interrupted my thoughts. It was the wolf mask again. The costume suited him perfectly. Steven was an old school chum of Eric's since before law school. The two were amazingly alike. Each was tall and dark and had that cutting ability to rankle one's composure.

"If you'll grant me just one dance I promise not to bother you anymore," he said.

I eyed him critically. "Very well."

He held me closer than was decent and smiled at me as if he knew my deepest, darkest secret. "I apologize for being such a pest, but Eric has done nothing but talk about you; so I had to see for myself what a treasure you really are."

"I see," I said. "And just what sort of things has Eric said about me?"

"Oh, no, I'm not about to divulge a friend's confidence. Let's just say he finds you intriguing. He's quite smitten, in fact."

"Really?" He apparently was not privy to all of Eric's confidences.

"Oh yes. And to be honest, at first I couldn't see the attraction."

"I beg your pardon?"

"I'm beginning to see it now. I've been watching you. You have a unique flair."

"I'll take that as a compliment."

"Please do. I mean it in the most flattering sense. In fact, if I was sure Eric wouldn't have my head for it, I might try for you myself."

"Don't I have any say in the matter?"

"Of course, what do you say? I don't want to influence you but I do have a great deal of money."

"So does Eric," I reminded him.

"Is that what he told you?" The man laughed out loud. "He's a sly one all right. I hate to break the news to you, but Eric is near penniless. The only thing his father left him is a mountain of debt. He worked nights as a bookkeeper to pay off most of it. He's just getting back on his feet now. He had to take out a mortgage on this place to cover the party."

I looked at him in disbelief.

"I'm sorry," he said with a touch of regret. "I guess I shouldn't have said anything. It looks as though Eric is going to have my head after all."

"No, that's all right. I promise not to say anything to him. It really doesn't matter anyway." Graham had some explaining to do. Where was he anyway? "Will you please excuse me. There's someone I must see."

"Yes, of course," he replied. "And I really am sorry."

I gave him a wan smile. He wasn't sorry in the least.

Where was Graham? I searched all the masks for that one familiar face but I couldn't find him. He was always late, but not like this. I looked at the clock. It was half past eleven. Almost midnight. He must be setting his trap for Eric in the cellar, I surmised.

I snatched a glass of champagne off a passing tray. It was my first all evening, something to calm my nerves. I took a sip and tried to relax. Eric was across the room playing the gallant host. He caught my eye and waved in silent greeting. He always seemed to be watching me. I turned my back and looked out the giant windows. How much longer could I go on pretending?

The clock ticked on. The guests were anxious for the time when they could remove their masks. For me it was the time to unmask the evil of Boothe House.

The full moon glowed brightly down on the ground below. It was a clear night. I could see from the gardens to the paddock and beyond. I could even see a slight reflection off the lake in the distance. The lake where Alicia Mae was found. Could hemlock have been the real cause of her death? Eric could have disguised it as a drowning. But where did he find the hemlock? I turned to look at the clock and then quickly back out the window again when I realized what I had just seen. Of course, why hadn't I thought of it before? I gazed down at the roof of the greenhouse. He didn't have to find it. It had been growing here all the time.

• TWENTY •

According to the clock it was twenty minutes to twelve. There was still time. I looked again at the greenhouse. It was attached to the house so there must be an entrance inside somewhere. I wound my way through the crowd to the door. While Eric was occupied I slipped out and down the stairs.

Guests flowed out of the ballroom onto the second floor. I tried to sneak past undetected. As I neared the foyer I heard the unmistakable voice of Aggie Towns. "No, his lordship didn't invite me. I'm a friend of Miss Barlow's," she told the befuddled butler. "If you don't mind, I'd like to see—"

"Aggie?" I called to her.

"Meredith? Is that you?"

I pulled off my mask. "It's me."

"Thank heavens! Would you mind telling this gentleman here who I am."

"It's all right," I assured the man. "She's a friend of mine." I showed Aggie to the library where we wouldn't be overheard. "What are you doing here?"

"A young girl from the house delivered this to me." She held out the note I had written. "You wrote here you solved the mystery and couldn't stay here anymore. I waited and waited, and when you didn't show up I told Duff to hook up the wagon."

"Oh Aggie, I have so much to tell you. But not here, not now. Is Duff with you?"

"He's waiting outside. He wouldn't come in. You know, the

208

house and all. Well, I'm glad to see that you're still in one piece and in such finery yet. You had me real worried. When you didn't show up at Sarah's funeral, bless her soul …" She paused to dab at her eyes. "I thought something might be wrong. Mr. Ferguson said there wasn't of course, but I tend not to believe everything he says—"

"Graham was there? He said nothing to me."

"Oh, he was there all right. I thought it odd you didn't come with him, you two being the last ones to visit her and all."

"How did you know I visited her that night?"

"I saw that machine of yours head out to her farm. It's kind of hard to miss, you know. You have to pass Croakers to get there."

"And what makes you think Graham was with me?"

"He passed right after you."

"But he never came to Sarah's."

She patted my hand. "Meredith, love, you don't have to pretend with me. I saw his motorcar follow you there. You told me how it was between you two. Remember?"

"But there's nothing between us. There never was. Are you sure it wasn't Eric's motorcar you saw?"

"Lord Boothe? Heavens no. I would recognize Ferguson anywhere. He took the same path he used to visit Alicia Mae. The Pruitt place neighbors Sarah's."

Graham had followed me that night? No wonder he was able to find me after the accident. I never thought to question it. Her words were beginning to sink in. "Wait, wait! What did you say? He used to visit Alicia Mae? Did Eric know about it?"

Aggie seemed confused at my questioning. "Well, I suppose he did. Their engagement was no secret."

"Whose engagement?"

"Ferguson and Alicia Mae's, of course."

I took Aggie by the shoulders and sat her down. "You mean to tell me Graham was going to marry Alicia and not Eric?"

"Well … yes. I told you she was to become the new mistress. It was common knowledge Ferguson became master of the house after the old Lord died. He made that quite clear enough. I think that's the reason why Alicia Mae wanted to marry him in the first place. Eric hadn't lived here for years. I don't think he even met her until just before she died."

"Oh, Aggie!"

"What's the matter, dear? You don't look well."

The pieces were falling into a neat little pattern. All the signs were there: Graham's devotion to his uncle and this house; the brake cable; the brandy—how many times had I seen him drink it? He was carrying on the legacy his uncle had left him. And the cellar. He wanted to ruin Eric the best way he knew how—through me.

"Oh Aggie, what have I done?" I cried.

The foyer clock began to chime one ... two ... three ... four ...

"What's that?"

"It's midnight I should think," Aggie replied. "Time you came home with me."

"Midnight!" The time Eric asked me to meet him.

The cellar. Graham! "I've got to stop him!"

"Wait," Aggie called after me. "Where are you off to now?"

There was no time to explain. I rushed through the kitchen to the back of the house and threw open the cellar door. "Eric?" He didn't answer. Was I too late?

There was a light streaming from somewhere down below. I grasped the banister firmly in hand and started a slow descent down the stairs. "Eric?"

The cellar door slammed shut. There was not a sound from below. My heart began to race. "Graham?"

The light grew brighter as I rounded a corner. Shelves lined the room stocked with wine and brandy—Edmund's brandy.

An elongated shadow moved upon the wall edging closer and closer. Masculine legs clad in tan stepped into view. The pirate. His stride was slow and uneven, his eyes glazed with shock. He stumbled, then fell into my arms. Blood trickled from his mouth. "I ... wanted ... to ... surprise ... you ..."

The gold scarf and eye patch fell to the ground. "Graham!" I placed a hand on his back to guide him to a chair. The hilt of a dagger met my palm. "Oh, my God! Graham!"

"I'm ... sorry ... I should ... have known ..." He crumbled to the floor. "Where's ..." His breath became short and labored.

"I'm going to get help. Don't move!"

I raced up the stairs to the cellar door. It was locked. My fists slammed into the wood. "Help us, please! Someone, please open the door!" I pounded and pounded until my hands felt numb and raw. "Is anyone there? Please, help us!" Muffled sounds of gaiety and laughter flowed down from high above. No one could hear me.

It all seemed surreal; everything moved in slow motion. Graham ... the knife ... the blood ... There was so much blood. *Was* Eric behind all this?

I returned to Graham's side. His brow was cold, his eyes void. And the dagger was gone.

Behind me a shadow crept along the floor, across my shoulder and over Graham's lifeless body.

"I never meant to kill him!" Linnea stood over me, blood on her hands, the dagger poised in midair.

"It was you?" But, of course, who else wanted to preserve the Boothe legacy. She adored Graham and would do anything for him. Even murder.

Tears dribbled down her cheeks. Her hair dangled unbound and unkempt in stringy lines over her face. She looked haggard and old. "My poor Graham. He dressed just like the bastard to please you. I didn't know." She fell to her knees to cradle his head in her lap. The dagger skidded across the floor. "I didn't know," she chanted. "Forgive me. Forgive me. My poor child." She rocked back and forth, stroking his pale brow and clutching him to her chest. "Yes, that's right. You rest now. I'll take care of everything. Haven't I always taken care of you? My dear, sweet Graham. It will be wonderful, you'll see. Boothe House will be yours just like you always wanted."

The woman had gone completely insane. I backed away toward the stairs to flee. The tall wig came undone and fell to the floor in a heap. My costume was heavy and awkward making me stumble on each step. When I reached the top I kicked and pounded on the door. "Help me! Please God! Will somebody help me?"

With a feral growl Linnea grabbed me from behind and pulled me down the stairs. The material of my gown tore from hip to hem. I lashed out with my limbs, but I was no match for Linnea's unnatural strength. She continued to drag me across the floor deep into the cellar and farther away from help.

"I knew you were going to cause trouble the moment you came," she spat, her eyes wide with madness. "You have to be stopped just like the others."

When I tried to stand, she hurled her small, but solid frame, against mine sending me crashing into the wall. The bricks scraped against my uncovered skin causing marks and drawing blood. Air whooshed from my lungs. "Why…?"

"Graham thought rumors of ghosts would scare the buyers away. It was working, too, until you came with your bright ideas. Then you found the journal. I always suspected that Eric was illegitimate. Graham thought he could use the information to claim Boothe House, but I knew it wouldn't work. I told him I would take care of it. I always took care of him. You led me to that Bradley woman, but she wouldn't talk. I swore she'd never talk again, but she didn't believe me." Linnea giggled, a sinister baneful sound. "What a fool! I'll wager she believes me now."

The horror of her deeds registered. Dear God, Sarah! "You used hemlock, didn't you?"

"Oh, yes," she answered with no remorse.

"And you knew it was in the brandy Eric gave me."

"Of course. Who do you think handed him the bottle? I just wanted to frighten you away. You were in no real danger. The recipe has been handed down for generations. The master taught me how to harvest the seedlings in early spring. We can have spring every day of the year in the greenhouse. I'm surprised you became as ill as you did, though. That brandy wasn't strong enough to harm you." She pulled a small vial of amber liquid from her pocket. "But this one is."

"Is that what Madelaine drank in her tea before you lured her down here?"

She bobbed her head. "It was all so simple. I followed the witch, Madelaine. I saw them together plotting their escape. I told the master they were going to steal his son. It was his idea to put the recipe in her tea. She followed me like a lamb. Such a dutiful mother she was."

It all became clear now: the brandy, the child-like figure luring Madelaine to her death, Sarah and Alicia. "You killed Alicia, too, didn't you?

"She betrayed my Graham. When Eric returned she set her sights on the real lord of the manor. She was going to break my poor Graham's heart. She had to be stopped. Just like you."

My heart raced painfully. I had to get out of there. I combed the brick walls looking for an escape. My fingers traced an outline of a door. The scent of sweet ginger permeated the bricks. I recoiled in terror. That was the room. Just beyond the wall was the place where Madelaine had taken her last breath. I turned my head away in disgust. "You'll never get away with it."

"My dear, wretched girl. I already have."

"Eric will come—"

"Oh, I hope so. I left him a note, too. Cinderella needs her Prince Charming. Hah! You think I didn't know? I know everything that goes on in this house. My Graham will finally take his rightful place as lord of the manor."

"Graham is dead, Linnea. You killed him, remember?"

She narrowed her eyes. "Graham? No, no, it was … I saw the costume … he called your name. He was standing right there … and I …" Linnea raised her arm in re-enactment. She shook her head. "No. Graham is upstairs waiting to announce Eric's illegitimacy at the party. He wanted to fool everybody. He was going to wear the same costume as …" She clutched her head. The memory was too much for her.

"He's dead," I repeated. "And you killed him, Linnea." I edged my way to the stairs. If I could just make someone hear me …

Linnea stood unsteady, rocking on her heels singing Graham's name over and over. Seizing my chance, I vaulted up the stairs. "Help me! Please, God! Somebody help me!"

"They won't come." Linnea's voice was deathly calm. She stood at the base of the stairs, the dagger gripped tightly in her hand.

I pounded and kicked wildly. "Please! Oh, God!"

The door shook with fury. "Meredith!"

"Eric!"

"He can't help you. The door is locked and I have the only key." Linnea lunged with the knife. I twisted to deflect the blow but her aim was true. The knife slashed through the gown and pierced my shoulder. Searing pain raced through my arm. Shock came next. *I really am going to die!*

"Nooo!"

"Meredith!" The heavy door rattled and shook.

Dear God! I'm going to die and no one can stop it. Oh, Eric! I never had the chance to tell you I loved you.

Linnea raised her arm for another assault. I grabbed her wrist. We struggled. I lost my balance and hit the stairs. Linnea tumbled with me. The knife bounced off the boards and clattered to the floor. At the bottom we rolled, over and over. My arms swung wildly in a futile effort to fend her off. She grabbed hold of my hair and gave it a painful twist.

My fingernails searched out the tender corners of her eyes. She screamed in outrage and released me. I crawled away but there was no where to turn. My shoulder ached. I felt dizzy and disoriented. Blood seeped through the once beautiful gown. It was warm, wet and sticky. *My blood.*

The knife lay under the last stair, a spec of silver glinting in the candlelight. I could see it. Linnea saw it, too. She reached for it just as the dumb waiter made a thundering crash.

Eric jumped out. His mask and scarf were gone. Sweat beaded his brow. "Meredith!" He sank to his knees. He touched my hair, my cheek, my hand. When he saw the blood, his eyes met mine. Fear—anger. He didn't understand it. But I did. I understood everything behind Boothe House now, especially how much I loved him.

"Eric … I'm sorry. I thought—"

"Shh. It doesn't matter now. We need to get you safe. Who—?"

From the corner of my eye I saw Linnea creep up behind Eric's back. The knife rose high in the air.

"Look out!" I yelled.

Eric turned just as the knife came down. The blade caught his temple. The small cut oozed red. His finger touched the spot. He stood looking down at Linnea in disbelief. She attacked again only this time Eric was prepared. He captured her wrist above her head and twisted her arm. Linnea cried out in agony. Slowly, the knife came down and slipped to the floor.

Incensed with rage, Linnea propelled herself toward Eric catching his throat in her hands. Eric sputtered once, caught his breath and backhanded the servant against the wall. I heard the contact as Linnea's head hit the bricks. She slumped to the floor, unconscious.

Eric came to my side.

"You're hurt," I said raising my hand to the wound at his temple.

He kissed my palm. "It's nothing. Graham?"

I shook my head. Tears began to flow uncontrollably. "He's dead. Linnea killed him. She thought he was you. Oh, Eric. I'm sorry—"

"Shh. You have nothing to be sorry about. Now let's get you out of here." He moved to lift me. Pain shot through my body in a thousand spasms. I sucked in my breath. Blood flowed freely from my shoulder.

"Christ! Hold on, Meredith!" He gathered me up and hurried up the stairs. He didn't notice it, but I did. The cellar door was open and Linnea was gone.

Their voices were muffled.

"No. They haven't found her yet, but they will. She couldn't have gone far."

"Well, I hope for your sake they do find that woman and soon. I gave Miss Barlow a sedative to help her sleep. She needed several stitches, but I think she'll pull through just fine. Here, let me have a look at that cut on your head …"

She came into the garden room quiet as a mouse. From her pocket, she removed a small vial. One drop, then two into the cup.

"Linnea!"

"Shh! Here drink this." Eric held the cup to my lips. "You were dreaming." The tea was hot and potent, but it felt oddly comforting.

The gown was gone. I was wrapped in blankets, but still I was cold, so very cold. Dr. Hathaway said it was the shock. The ball had come to an abrupt end. All the guests had left except for Dr. Hathaway. The servants hurried to clean up and be gone— away from Boothe House. It was well past dawn. How long had I been asleep? "A dream?"

"Not surprising after what you've been through. Take another sip. It will warm you up."

He had changed out of his pirate costume into brown trousers and a cream shirt. A bandage covered one eyebrow down to his cheekbone. "Your head!"

"It's fine," he assured me. "Just a few stitches. It will leave a scar though."

"The women will be swooning in the streets," I said and meant it. Eric was enticingly handsome. A scar would only add to the mystery.

"I'm only concerned about one woman." He leaned down and brushed his lips against my forehead. "I told Mrs. Towns that you would see her in a few days. She's a very persistent woman. I had to swear to your safety on bended knee before she would leave."

I smiled. That was Aggie for you. Dear ole Aggie. If it hadn't been for her I never would have learned the truth. "I'm sorry Eric. Can you ever forgive me for doubting you?"

"There's nothing to forgive. I should be apologizing to you. I knew Graham was behind the rumors; then after your accident I thought he had completely lost control. The man at the garage told me your brake cable was cut. I never suspected Linnea."

"Neither did I. Oh, Eric! She killed them all—Alicia, Sarah, Graham …" And Madelaine. Should I tell him? I wondered. Should I tell Eric the truth about his mother and father? She had known. Madelaine had known about the danger. She tried to tell me, but I just didn't see it. She hadn't come to me in an effort to unveil the truth; she came to protect Eric from Edmund's evil influence. And I had almost failed her. "She killed your mother, too. Down in the cellar. Your father had—"

"My mother? What are you talking about?"

"Eric there's something I have to tell you. I've been having these dreams … and then I found this journal …" A strange twinge caught my stomach. I paused to rub the pain away.

"What's the matter?" he asked.

"I don't feel very well."

"It's all the excitement. You're tired and confused. Just put your head back and rest now. We can tell me all about it later."

"But I have to tell you—" Another cramp took hold. I

groaned.

"Is it your stomach?"

I nodded with a grimace.

"You haven't had anything to eat, have you?"

"No, all I've had was the sedative Dr. Hathaway gave me and the tea ..." *It wasn't a dream!* "Oh God, Eric!" I gripped his arm. "The tea! Linnea was in here. It wasn't a dream!"

"Don't move," he ordered.

"Wait! Where are you going? Don't leave me."

"I'm going to get Dr. Hathaway."

The cramps moved down to my legs. "Dear God, no!" I cried. Linnea was going to have her revenge after all.

Eric was back moments later with Dr. Hathaway. "Try and relax Meredith," the good doctor said. "This is going to be uncomfortable."

He began pulling tubes and bottles out of his bag.

Terror took hold. "Eric!"

He reached for my hand. "I'm here sweetheart."

"I'm going to die, aren't I?"

"No! I won't let that happen. I promise." His lips felt hot against my brow. He looked into my eyes. "I love you, Meredith. You have to hold on."

Having my stomach evacuated was not an experience I wished to remember, but it saved my life. Linnea's disappearance was a mystery. Eric promised they would find her. I believed him.

The house had quieted by the following evening. I found Eric by the fire in the library with Madelaine's journal in his lap. He was so immersed in thought he didn't hear me approach.

I placed a comforting hand on his shoulder. He looked startled for a moment. "What are you doing out of bed? You are in no condition to be roaming the house. Here, come sit." He set the journal on the table and pulled me onto his lap.

I wrapped my robe closer around my bandaged shoulder and

snuggled close against his chest. "I thought you'd left." I didn't want to say that until Linnea was caught I was afraid to be alone.

We sat quietly looking into the fire. Eric's eyes strayed to the portrait of his mother. He remained silent.

"I'm sorry," I said. "You must have loved your father very much."

"Loved him? I hated him. The man had no idea how to be a real father. He was much too busy festering his hate for my mother. The only thing I'm grateful to him for is for sending me away to school. I spent most of my life apart from Boothe House. For that I have no regrets. Except one." He stared at his mother's portrait.

"She really did love you, you know."

"Yes," he sighed. "I know that now. She was a remarkable woman. Do you know she had me convinced that I was allergic to the berries my father used in his brandy? She made me swear never to drink any of it. And I never did."

"I think she'll rest at peace now, knowing you're safe and know the truth. Why are you looking at me like that? You still don't believe your mother's spirit came to me in my dreams, do you?"

His lips turned up in a crooked smile. "Of course I believe you. I think she made an excellent choice."

"You don't believe me. I can tell. You think I created the entire thing in my head."

"I've always admired your imagination."

"And did I imagine the part where you said you loved me?"

His expression turned serious. "No." Then he smiled. "That was reality at its best."

He was truly a beast of perfection. My heart fluttered in my chest. "Maybe you should explain to me what is reality and what is an illusion."

"My pleasure. This is reality." His lips stroked my temple. "And this." He kissed my cheek and my nose. "This, too." His mouth centered over mine and let nature take its course. After several glorious minutes, I pushed against his chest. We were moving way too fast down a strange road that seemed to have no end. "And illusion?" I asked.

"The illusion is in believing I would ever leave you. I love you, Meredith. You once asked me what my weakness is. It's you, and it scares the hell out of me."

"It scares me, too. I've never been in love before."

"Then how do you know you are?" he posed.

"I know because when I'm with you I feel complete and delightfully alive. And when you're gone I'm overcome with an insane jealousy thinking you're with someone else."

"You do?"

I nodded. "Who is Paulette?"

"Paulette?" He laughed, but I didn't think it so very humorous. "She's no one."

"Prove it."

"Gladly." He leaned me over until my hair brushed the floor. Blood raced to my injured shoulder. I winced.

He straightened, contrite. "Sorry. I'll be more careful next time."

"You're so sure there's going to be a next time."

His smile turned intensely seductive. "Positive."

I felt the prediction right down to my toes. *Lord, I hate it when he's always right.*

"Come, let's get you back to bed." He lifted me effortlessly in his arms.

"You're going to carry me all the way to the bedroom."

He bent a grin. "I've fantasized about nothing else."

I laughed. "You are a wicked man, Eric Boothe."

"Flattery will get you everywhere, my dear."

Ana knocked on the door. "I'm sorry to disturb you, sir," she said. "But there's a man at the door who claims to be a colonel."

"My father!"

Eric's eyebrow rose in wonder. "To what do we owe this unexpected pleasure?"

"I have no idea," I said, coming into a panic. "Why would he come all this way ... Oh, for pity sake! I forgot to write!"

"Not very obedient of you but hardly a reason to bring him all the way up here."

"You don't know the Colonel. Put me down. If he sees us like this he'll—"

"He'll what? Demand that I marry you?"

I nodded. "Something like that."

Eric sighed and held me tight. "Then I'll just have to beat him to it, won't I? Show the gentleman in, Ana. I think it's time I met my future father-in-law."

I beamed. Who said he wasn't the perfect hero?

❧ EPILOGUE ❦

Madelaine's story, *A Journey of Fate* was published six months later. I exercised my poetic license to change the ending to a happy one. Eric approved. I believe Madelaine would have, too.

They found Madelaine's and Eric Jeffries' remains in the secret room of the cellar. They were put to rest side by side in the Hemlock cemetery next to Sarah and Ian. Eric wouldn't have it any other way.

Graham was buried in the family crypt next to Edmund and the rest of the Boothe ancestors. Linnea never returned to the house. She was found a week after the ball of an apparent suicide, the vial of hemlock still clutched in her hand.

The greenhouse was torn down and burned. Boothe House itself still stands though we have yet to return there. Vines and thorns have reestablished themselves along the perimeter of the house. Pieces of brick and mortar have fallen again. It no longer resembles the fine house Eric restored it to be. A sign is posted near the road offering it for sale. That, too, has been swallowed by the invading landscape.

I am told Ignacious still roams the roads outside Boothe House, and the sound of Edmund's laughter can be heard when the wind is just right. They say a light appears now and then, and a figure of a man is seen standing guard by a window, watching for any persons who'd be so foolish as to trespass there. This light burns brightest in the room Graham once lived in.

The legacy lives on.

About the Author

Eden Reed

Eden first started penning stories in the sixth grade. But it wasn't until she opened a gothic mystery many years later that she fell in love with reading. The puzzling who-done-it caught her interest, and before long she was writing her first novel. She decided to combine her love of old movies with the intrigue of mystery for *Valley of Hemlock*. The story is a classic tale of good vs. evil but with an added twist readers are sure to find irresistible.

When she is not writing fiction novels Eden works as a freelance journalist. Her work has been published in numerous magazines and newspapers across the country. Eden is currently working on her next suspense novel. She lives outside of Chicago with her husband and two children. Readers may write to her at:

Eden Reed
c/o New Leaf Books
P.O. Box 6992
Villa Park, IL 60181

edenareed@newleafbooks.net

www.ingramcontent.com/pod-product-compliance
Lightning Source LLC
Chambersburg PA
CBHW020409180626
46812CB00003B/892